"I'm a thief,

"It won't matter what
coerced you and toss

"Not without proof they won't."

"Since when do they need proof to arrest someone?"

"I don't know what happened with your arrest," she admitted. "But you don't have to worry about tonight."

Dante slanted her a glance. "There's still one problem."

"What?"

"I don't believe *you*."

He didn't believe she'd stand up for him? "Why not?"

"Why should I?"

"Because I said I would. And my word is good."

"You've been lying to me from the start."

"The reason I need that tape doesn't matter."

"It matters. I'm in this mess as much as you are, so you damned well owe me the truth. And until I get it, I'm not letting you out of my sight."

"What?"

"You heard me, princess. You're stuck with me until I decide I'm out."

★ ★ ★

Dear Reader,

I love edgy heroes. The more cynical, disillusioned and bitter they are, the more they fascinate me. That's why I invented the Stealth Knights—heroes who straddle that murky line between right and wrong, who are neither all good nor all bad, and who prove that nothing in life is as clear-cut as it seems.

The hero of *High-Stakes Affair,* Dante Quevedo, is one such complicated man. A modern-day Robin Hood, Dante dedicates his life to righting the injustices done to his downtrodden people, albeit through unorthodox means. But when circumstances force him to team up with his sworn enemy, Princess Paloma Vergara, he discovers she isn't the frivolous royal he believed—and that the woman who once seemed completely wrong for him might instead be exactly right.

I hope you enjoy this latest installment in the Stealth Knights miniseries. Happy reading!

Gail Barrett

GAIL BARRETT

High-Stakes Affair

ROMANTIC
SUSPENSE

Recycling programs
for this product may
not exist in your area.

ISBN-13: 978-0-373-27767-4

HIGH-STAKES AFFAIR

Copyright © 2012 by Gail Ellen Barrett

Books by Gail Barrett

Harlequin Romantic Suspense

Cowboy Under Siege #1672
‡*High-Risk Reunion* #1682
‡*High-Stakes Affair* #1697

Silhouette Romantic Suspense

Facing the Fire #1414
*Heart of a Thief #1514
*To Protect a Princess #1538
His 7-Day Fiancée #1560
*The Royal Affair #1601
Meltdown #1610

Silhouette Special Edition

Where He Belongs #1722

*The Crusaders
‡Stealth Knights

Other titles by this author available in ebook format.

GAIL BARRETT

always knew she'd be a writer. Who else would spend her childhood grinding sparkling rocks into fairy dust and convincing her friends it was real? Or daydream her way through elementary school, spend high school reading philosophy and playing the bagpipes, then head off to Spain during college to live the writer's life? After four years she straggled back home—broke, but fluent in Spanish. She became a teacher, earned a master's degree in linguistics, married a coast guard officer and had two sons.

But she never lost the desire to write. Then one day she discovered a Silhouette Intimate Moments novel in a bookstore—and knew she was destined to write romance. Her books have won numerous awards, including a National Readers' Choice Award and Romance Writers of America's prestigious Golden Heart.

Gail currently lives in western Maryland. Readers can contact her through her website, www.gailbarrett.com.

To Liz and Amanda, for making my sons so happy.

Acknowledgments

I'd like to thank the following people for their enormous help with this story: Loni Glover for her emergency brainstorming sessions; Ken Archer for providing me with accounting details; Elle Kennedy for her much-needed encouragement; Judith Sandbrook and Mary Jo Archer for their invaluable critiques; and last but not least, my husband, John, for not complaining when I went AWOL to finish this book.

Chapter 1

If there was one thing Dante Quevedo knew intimately, it was revenge. He'd lived it, breathed it and plotted it for twenty years. And tonight it would finally be his.

He pressed the trigger on the remote control detonator, then watched as a potent mixture of C-4 and diesel fuel exploded, shooting brilliant orange flames high into the midnight sky and rumbling the ground beneath his feet. With a quick surge of satisfaction, he slid the detonator back into his knapsack, then slipped through the inky shadows to the machinery shed where the casino's emergency generators were housed.

The bomb's fire leaped and roared in the darkness. Security guards rushed past, shouting into their radios as they raced toward the rocketing blaze. Dante crept around the shed, the thick smoke shielding his movements from the surveillance cameras mounted on the walls, and paused at the metal door. Using his custom-made stainless-steel diamond pick, he jimmied the lock and stepped inside.

He glanced at his watch. *Sixteen minutes*. Not much time to disable the backup generators and get himself in place. Then the hacker would work his computer magic and cut the main power to the casino, allowing Dante to break into the penthouse, the aristocrat who'd hired him in tow.

Misgivings stirred inside him, but he shook them off. He'd agreed to the deal—his release from prison in exchange for getting the unknown woman inside. Her reasons, her goal—hell, even her identity—didn't matter.

Only Dante's chance for vengeance did.

Resolve fisting deep inside him, he strode to the generators' control panel, located the power switch and turned it off. Then he sawed through the fuel lines with his wire cutters and opened the drains on the tanks to buy more time. Diesel fuel poured out, the harsh fumes stinging his nostrils and watering his eyes. Knowing time was dwindling quickly, he returned to the door and peered outside.

Smoke still billowed past. A cacophony of sirens pierced the air as emergency vehicles sped up the Pyrenees mountain slope. His adrenaline rising, Dante stepped from the shed and locked the door, then melted into the night.

Picking up his pace now, he jogged to the stolen hatchback he'd parked at the periphery of the gravel lot. *Nine minutes*. He opened the trunk, tugged a crisp white dress shirt over his T-shirt, then yanked on his jacket and tie. Still hurrying, he stuffed his lock-picking tools into his pocket, brushed the leaves and twigs from his suit trousers, and stowed his knapsack beneath a nearby shrub. If all hell broke loose, he didn't want any evidence traced to him.

Moving slower to avoid attention, he strolled casually past the valet parking and up the casino's wide stone steps. Located in a medieval fortress, País Vell's opulent playground attracted high rollers from around the world. Dante nodded to the uniformed doorman, stepped into the chandelier-studded lobby and paused.

The domed ceiling soared above him. Huge marble columns shouldered the mezzanine, its gilded railing glinting in the refracted light. Bells jangled from the adjacent gaming pit, the cheerful noise razoring through him like a garrote to his heart. His sister Lucía had died in this casino. She would never laugh, never hear those sounds again.

He steeled his jaw against a rush of emotions, guilt over his failure to save her bludgeoning his heart. Her death haunted him, all right. He couldn't stop reliving her final, frantic phone call—that she needed him to help her, that the prince was trying to kill her, that she had witnessed something dreadful during her waitressing shift and had to leave. Dante had raced to the casino, only to find her body dumped in the parking lot like discarded trash. Bloody. Mutilated.

Dead.

He closed his eyes and inhaled deeply, the burning need for vengeance threatening to incinerate his hardwon control. But he'd get revenge; he had no doubts about that. He'd find the evidence he needed to destroy the prince—and every other member of the royal family—no matter what it took.

But he had a bargain to fulfill first.

Still careful not to attract attention, he stalked across the marble lobby to the gaming pit, then wove past the baccarat tables and roulette wheels to the private high-limit rooms off the palace's central hall. He checked his watch. *Five minutes.* The aristocrat would be in one of the high-roller rooms by now. The plan called for her to enter the hallway nearest the medieval watchtower a minute before the power went off. Dante estimated they'd have half an hour to break into the penthouse, find whatever she wanted and return to the hallway before the maintenance people restored the power.

Veering past a display of medieval armor, he headed to a nearby restroom and ducked inside. *Two minutes.* He drew in a breath, mentally reviewing the palace's layout as another minute ticked down.

His belly tensed. A familiar surge of excitement drummed through his veins. One minute left. The game was on.

He stepped back into the hall.

Right on schedule, a woman sauntered down the hall toward him, her slender hips swiveling in her snug black pants, her long legs covering the distance with graceful strides. Dante took in her firm, high breasts, her sweetly curving waist. Thick dark hair cascaded around her shoulders, gleaming like burnished chestnuts in the muted light.

He knit his brows, something about her niggling his memory, prompting a feeling of familiarity he couldn't place. He shrugged the sensation off. He couldn't possibly know her. He had little contact with País Vell's wealthy elite—except when he broke into their estates, relieving them of their cash and jewels.

Conscious of the surveillance cameras recording his movements, he turned toward the water fountain—just as a man strode behind her into the hall.

Dante's heart skipped. He eyed the newcomer's short,

burly build, the bulge of a sidearm beneath his suit, the hyperalert way he scanned the hall. *A bodyguard.* What the hell? No one had mentioned him.

Suspicions crowding inside him, Dante leaned over the fountain and dipped his head to drink. This couldn't be a trap; why bother springing him from prison only to arrest him again? Besides, he trusted his friend Rafael Navarro, the former thief who'd arranged this deal. Rafe never would have set him up.

But then who was the unknown aristocrat? Why would she bring a bodyguard along? And what the hell was he going to do now?

He took several long swallows of water, waiting until the woman had nearly reached him, then angled her another glance. His eyes connected with hers, and recognition kicked him straight in the gut.

Paloma Vergara.

The princess.

His jaw slackened in disbelief.

But it was her, all right. He could hardly mistake her infamous oval face, those mesmerizing amber eyes. He scanned her dark winged brows, her sinfully carnal mouth, that elegant, fine-boned jaw. She continued gliding toward him, her head held high, her slender spine erect, centuries of privilege and breeding evident in every regal step.

A hot rush of fury scorched his gut. No wonder Rafe had kept her name a secret. If Dante had known her identity, he never would have agreed to this job. The royals had gunned down his helpless mother. They'd murdered his baby sister. There wasn't a chance in hell he'd help anyone even remotely connected to them.

And this princess… He thinned his lips in disgust. Paloma Vergara was a notorious wild child, a pampered, frivolous tabloid queen whose escapades had outraged the nation for years. She spent her useless life partying, squandering money earned on the backs of the down-trodden people—epitomizing everything he despised.

She drew even closer, her gaze locked on his. Suddenly, she stumbled, a flash of uncertainty flickering in her eyes. But she recovered her poise and strolled through the door of the women's lounge, trailing a taunting wisp of perfume.

His face muscles rigid, anger pounding his veins with the force of that bomb blast, Dante turned back to the fountain and swore. He should call this off. He should walk away right now. She was the princess, his enemy, a member of the family he'd sworn to destroy. And now he had her bodyguard to contend with, a complication that could get him killed.

But he'd promised to take her into the penthouse in exchange for his release from jail. The princess had done her part and freed him, so how could he renege on the deal?

He scowled at the gurgling water, an onslaught of conflicting emotions waging a full-blown war in his head. Every survival instinct he possessed urged him to get out now. But his word meant everything to him. His lifestyle might not be conventional—stealing from the aristocrats to help País Vell's poorest citizens—but he followed his own strict code of honor, meting out justice and revenge.

Abort the mission or adjust? He had only seconds left to decide.

He took a final swallow of water. The princess's bodyguard stopped, taking up his post beside the restroom door. *Ten seconds.* Dante continued debating his choices, but a grim feeling of inevitability settled inside. Bottom line, he'd given his word. He had to complete this mission, no matter what.

Hoping to hell he wouldn't regret this, he turned off the fountain and prepared to strike.

Princess Paloma Vergara had done plenty of things she wasn't proud of in her life. She'd shown up drunk at a state dinner. She'd had an affair with a man who'd turned out to be a foreign spy. She'd even appeared naked on the internet, thanks to a particularly sleazy boyfriend with a hidden telephoto lens.

But breaking into the casino penthouse was a new low, even for her.

Leaning against the wall inside the restroom, she pressed her palm to her belly to suppress a burst of nerves. But she could hardly miss the irony. She'd been trying for years to rehabilitate her image, to overcome a lifetime spent disappointing her family and finally prove her worth. Now she was about to obliterate a decade of progress with just one act.

But she was desperate. She *had* to get into that penthouse and confiscate the blackmail evidence tonight. The casino owner would destroy the prince's reputation—and possibly the entire monarchy—if she failed.

And better that *she* do this than her brother Tristan. At least if she got caught, no one would blink. Her reputation had been ruined years ago.

Nothing would go wrong, she reminded herself fiercely. This thief, Dante Quevedo, was reputed to be the best. He'd sneak her into the penthouse to find the incriminating surveillance footage and whisk her safely back out.

More anxiety swirled inside her at the thought of the man loitering in the hallway, the memory of his stark, dark face and furious eyes bringing a rush of heat to her skin. She'd expected someone older, shorter…more manageable.

But Dante Quevedo… She swallowed hard. He was too big, too male, *too dangerous*. He radiated testosterone and power. And the hostility in his midnight eyes…

She inhaled deeply, refusing to let him unsettle her. So he wasn't what she'd expected. Tough. No matter how much he disturbed her, she couldn't back out now.

She glanced at her watch. *Two seconds.* Her heartbeat accelerating, she straightened and faced the door.

The lights winked out. The casino's mechanical systems powered down, a sudden unnatural hush descending on the pitch-black air.

Her tension rising, Paloma swung open the restroom door and stepped back into the hall—just as a sickening thud reached her ears.

She cringed. She'd hoped her bodyguard Carlos would wait for her down the hall. But if he'd interfered and hurt the thief… What was she going to do now?

A tiny light flickered on. The narrow beam of a penlight drew her gaze to the floor—where Carlos lay slumped at Dante's feet.

Her jaw dropped. Carlos was an expert fighter. How had this thief managed to take him down?

"What did you do?" she cried, rushing to him. "You didn't hurt him?" The last thing she wanted was to cause her protector harm.

"He's fine. He'll just have a headache when he comes to." Dante's flinty eyes narrowed on hers. "But what's with the bodyguard? He wasn't part of our deal."

"I know. I'm sorry. I tried to sneak off without him, but he wouldn't let me out of his sight."

Dante only grunted in answer, then held his penlight out. "Here. Hold this."

Still staggered at Dante's prowess, she grabbed the penlight and aimed it his way. His back muscles flexed under his suit coat as he gripped Carlos beneath his arms and dragged him across the hall.

"Open the door," he ordered, his deep voice rumbling in the dark.

Feeling even more off-kilter, she opened the restroom door. Dante dumped Carlos inside and reached for the penlight again. "Let's go. We don't have much time."

"Right." They had to hurry to commit a crime.

He strode down the hallway, the small light bobbing in the dark. Her sense of unreality mounting, Paloma scurried behind him, trying to keep up with his lengthy strides. Disembodied voices floated through the darkness—casino workers running through nearby corridors, rushing to restore the power.

But her thoughts kept returning to the bodyguard sprawled on the restroom floor. What would he do when he regained consciousness? Would he assume she'd been abducted and raise the alarm? And what if she and Dante got arrested? What if she couldn't find the blackmailer's evidence, and the royal family was ruined?

Fighting back a flurry of anxiety, she rushed after Dante down a private hall. This plan would work. It had to. She'd find that computer disk and return to the hallway before the power came back on. She had too much riding on this to fail.

Dante stopped at the tower door. A remnant of the medieval stronghold, the circular, three-story watchtower led to the penthouse, where the casino owner, César Gomez, had his private suite. Dante tugged on a pair of gloves and swung open the door.

She shot him a look of surprise. "It wasn't locked?"

"It's electronic. That's why we cut the power."

Of course. Completely out of her depth now, she followed him through the door. He led the way up the spiral stone staircase, taking the steps two at a time. She hurried after, her nerves coiling tighter as they neared the penthouse floor.

Would Gomez be at home? That was the million-dollar question, the one she'd been trying to answer all night. He hadn't answered her phone calls. His employees hadn't seen him in days. She prayed he'd left town on an impromptu vacation, because if he found her snooping through his penthouse...

She swallowed hard. It didn't matter. No matter what the danger, she had to take the risk. It was pointless to pay a blackmailer to stay silent; his demands would only get worse.

And she didn't dare let him expose that surveillance footage. Not now. Not with the country on edge. The sight of her brother partying with an international terrorist—no matter how innocent his actions had been— would further anger the citizens, leading to even more violent unrest.

They reached the fire door at the top of the staircase, and Dante paused again. "Wait here until I check it out."

Nodding her agreement, she leaned against the wall to catch her breath.

Dante opened the door and peeked out. "It's clear. Come on."

Her pulse skittering wildly, she followed him from the stairwell into a wide stone vestibule carpeted with Belgian rugs. To the right stood Gomez's private elevator, now dark. On the left loomed the door to the penthouse suite, its heavy planks covered with iron studs.

Experiencing another burst of anxiety, she glanced around, the ominous silence fueling her doubts. Because if anyone got wind of this break-in…

But she was committed now.

Dante handed her the penlight again. "Hold this while I pick the lock."

"I thought the locks were electronic."

"This one has a battery backup."

That made sense. "You need the light?" she asked, shining it at the door.

"No." Tugging two metal picks from his coat pocket, he lowered himself to one knee. Then he inserted the tools in the lock and closed his eyes.

Paloma shot another nervous glance behind her, then returned her attention to the thief, taking in his hard, chiseled mouth, his flat, masculine cheekbones, his thick shock of straight black hair. He probed the lock by feel, his big hands surprisingly gentle as he worked the picks, intense focus etched on his handsome face.

No, not handsome, she amended. His features were too strong for that, his nose a little too crooked. He was… virile. Blatantly and unapologetically male. She skimmed the cords of his sinewed neck, the impossible breadth of his shoulders, the black beard scruff shadowing his jaw.

She experienced a wayward thrill.

She stiffened, shocked. She could *not* be attracted to this man. He was a thief, a common criminal. And she'd worked far too hard to subdue her wild streak to back-slide into temptation now.

The lock gave way. Motioning for her to be quiet, Dante rose and cracked open the door. He listened for a moment, his ear to the small opening, then signaled for her to follow. Trying to keep her mind off Dante and on the job she needed to do, she slipped inside.

A feeling of *wrongness* instantly struck her. She glanced around the penthouse, intense dread gathering at the base of her spine, but nothing appeared out of place. Moonlight filtered through the deep-set windows. A profound stillness gripped the suite, assuring her that they were alone. She scanned the grand piano rising like a phantom in the moonlight, a huge dining-room table with high-backed medieval chairs.

Of course she'd feel jittery. She'd never committed a crime before. What did she expect?

"What are you looking for?" Dante asked, his voice low.

She opened her mouth to tell him, then stopped. The blackmailer was targeting her brother. It was Tristan's secret to reveal, not hers.

Impatience flashed in Dante's eyes. "Look, Princess. We've only got a few minutes until the power comes on, and I don't intend to be here when it does."

She couldn't afford to get caught, either. And two people could search faster than one. "I'm looking for a computer disk."

"What's on it?"

His blunt question caught her off guard. "Does it matter?"

"If I'm going to steal something, I'd like to know why."

"We're not stealing. Not really," she added when he shot her a look of disbelief. "It's footage from a surveillance camera. It has something…incriminating on it. Blackmail evidence."

Dante snorted.

She blinked, his skepticism taking her aback. "You don't believe me?"

"Hardly."

"But...why not?"

"Because it's ridiculous, that's why. Why would anyone blackmail you? Your reputation's already bad."

His obvious disdain made her face burn, but she couldn't argue his point. The tabloids had bad-mouthed her for years—and rightfully so. She'd made so many mistakes since childhood that País Vell's citizens despised her now.

And no matter how hard she tried to redeem herself—no matter how many charities she funded, no matter how many hours she volunteered each week at the royal hospital, doing everything from fundraising and reading to patients, to entertaining the children in the pediatric ward—she couldn't change their minds.

Which was exactly why she was here. She knew better than anyone the damage a bad reputation could do. And she refused to let that happen to her brother, Tristan, the heir to País Vell's throne.

She raised her chin. "I'm telling you the truth. I'm trying to stop a blackmailer, whether you want to believe me or not. Now, I suggest we get to work."

Dante didn't move. His gaze stayed clamped on hers, his skepticism clear. Then his eyes shifted to her mouth and heated with sensual awareness, making her pulse go berserk.

So he felt the attraction, too.

But his mouth hardened into a scowl. "Have it your way, Princess." He slapped the penlight into her hand. "You check the cabinets. I'll look for a safe. Did you bring gloves?"

"Yes." Her voice came out breathless. Her heart racketing around her rib cage, she pulled a pair of leather gloves from her back pocket and put them on. *Wrong man. Wrong time. Definitely the wrong place,* she reminded herself sternly. She had to concentrate on finding that computer disk, not let her unruly hormones lead her astray—no matter how compelling Dante was.

He disappeared into the shadows. Still badly rattled, she forced her attention to the suite. Starting at the nearby wet bar, she searched the liquor cabinet and cupboards, then continued around the room. The dining area yielded nothing. Neither did the sideboard, the closet in the spacious bedroom or the bedside table drawers. Kneeling, she shone the penlight under the bed. Nothing, not even dust.

Her desperation growing, she rose. That computer disk *had* to be here, and she had to find it tonight. But she was fast running out of time.

She spotted Dante searching the office and headed his way, catching up with him at Gomez's desk. "I doubt he'd keep it here," she said, but she rifled through a drawer, just in case. "It's too obvious."

"You'd be surprised what people do. Half the time they install safes, then don't even bother to put their valuables inside."

She paused at that, his words a stark reminder that she hardly knew this man. She knew he owned a small stone-masonry business on the edge of town. He was supposedly a thief, which his actions tonight confirmed. She'd even heard rumors that he might be El Fantasma, the Ghost, a modern-day Robin Hood who plagued the aristocrats of País Vell. And he'd spent the past two weeks locked up in the royal prison, although with his arrest record oddly missing, no one seemed to know why.

She shook her head. Dante's background didn't matter, not with that damaging surveillance footage threatening the security of País Vell. But neither could she afford to discount his expert advice. In case Gomez *had* left the incriminating evidence in the open, she fished a plastic bag from his wastepaper basket, then scooped up every flash drive and computer disk she spotted, no matter what their labels said.

"I need the light," Dante said from across the room. He swung aside a wall painting, exposing a safe.

He'd found it. Relief spiraling through her, she rushed around the desk.

"Aim it at the keypad," he added.

Moving in even closer, she complied. But standing this near, the heat from his muscled body teasing her senses, she couldn't keep her gaze off him. She skimmed his short, tousled hair, the grooves bracketing his sensual mouth, the black beard shadow coating his throat. Another shimmer of awareness fluttered through her, and she dragged in a calming breath. There was something riveting about this man, something that appealed to her in a basic, primal way.

Something she had no business indulging in right now.

Not ever. She'd put an end to her rebellious streak and sworn off inappropriate men. She had a duty to her country to fulfill.

Dante's long, lean fingers tapped the keypad. The safe popped open, and he edged the door aside.

"That was fast," she said.

"He's sloppy. He's worn off the numbers on the keys he uses most, so it was easy to figure out. And I got lucky. These electronic keypads go into lockdown if you enter four invalid codes. I got it right in three."

Not sure whether to be impressed or appalled, she peered into the open safe. But all she saw was a stack of ledgers, and her hopes instantly tanked. "That disk has to be here." She couldn't keep the desperation from her voice.

Dante glanced at his watch. "I'll look in the bathroom while you check. Then we need to go. We're cutting it close as it is."

Not wasting any time, she took out the stack of ledgers and searched the safe. She found a bag of antique coins, a few pairs of diamond cuff links—but no computer disk. Cursing César Gomez, she held the ledgers by their spines and shook them, in case the disk was wedged inside.

A tiny manila envelope fell to the floor. Bending down, she picked it up and looked inside. It was a key—but to what? Obviously not this safe. Unless there was another one in the room? But surely Dante would have found it by now.

On the off chance that it mattered, she stuffed the key into the bag with the computer disks, replaced the ledgers and closed the safe. Then she headed to the bathroom, her last resort. But as she stepped inside, Dante hustled over and blocked her way, forcing her to stumble back out. "What are you doing?" she asked, trying to go around him.

"Don't go in there."

"Why not? I need to—" A horrible stench wafted past, and she gagged. *Oh, God.* "Is it Gomez? Is he—?"

"Yeah, he's dead."

Shock rippled through her. She grabbed hold of the door frame, unable to catch her breath. "Dead?" she repeated, dumbfounded. "But that's impossible." He'd been alive two days ago, when he'd telephoned her brother, demanding cash. "Let me see."

"You don't want to go in there. It's bad."

"How bad? Was he murdered?"

His eyes grim, Dante shook his head.

"Suicide?"

"Worse."

"Worse than suicide?" A deep sense of trepidation clawed her throat. What could be worse than that? "Please," she whispered. "I need to know."

His eyes turning even grimmer, he took her bag from her trembling hands and stepped away.

Foreboding turning her blood cold, she took a deep breath and went inside.

Chapter 2

Paloma inched her way into the bathroom, fear beating against her breastbone like a vulture's wings, the narrow beam from the penlight wavering on the marble floor. She held her breath, one hand clamped over her mouth and nose as she tried not to inhale the fetid stench.

An unnatural silence drummed around her. The soft thud of her footsteps echoed in the gloom. Keeping her gaze trained on the wobbling penlight, she crept past an Iranian granite vanity, a shower big enough to dance in, an enormous ivory stone bathtub shaped like a giant egg.

The beam struck a man's bare foot, and she stopped. Her heart revving fast enough for liftoff, she swept the light over his pajama-clad body, then blinked, struggling to process the sight.

It was Gomez, all right. He lay flat on his back in a pool of blood. More blood had run across the floor tiles, settling in the grout lines like a macabre maze. And his face…

Her stomach roiled. A wild sound escaped her throat. His skin had puffed up, as if trying to separate from his body. He'd bled from every opening—his nose, his mouth, his ears. Even worse, a bizarre rash covered his face like mutant tapioca pudding, large patches of it forming purple shadows across his cheeks and jaw. His open eyes were a shocking, unnerving red.

Bile instantly mushroomed inside her. She spun on her heels, raced around the corner to the toilet and retched, unable to believe what she'd seen. What on earth had killed him? What caused that grotesque rash? A disease? But what? And the color of his eyes…

She vomited again, repeatedly, until the violent spasms gave way to dry heaves. Her legs threatening to collapse, she flushed the toilet, then staggered to the vessel sink nearest the door. She snapped off her gloves, turned on a sleek chrome faucet studded with Swarovski crystals, and cupped her hands to rinse her mouth, so shocked she could hardly think.

Dante appeared beside her. His eyes connected with hers in the shadowed mirror. "Are you all right?"

Her knees trembling madly, she grabbed hold of the vanity and shook her head. "I've never…I've never seen anything so awful. All that blood…" Her head grew light, and she swayed.

Swearing, he lunged toward her. He grabbed her arm, towed her outside the bathroom and slammed the door, walling off the disgusting smell. Then he wrapped his arms around her and pushed her head against his chest. "Breathe," he ordered, his voice gruff.

Too badly shaken to protest, she clutched the lapel of his suit coat, taking refuge in his strength and warmth.

Gomez's death had been worse than suicide, all right. But what *was* it? What could have caused those demonically red eyes?

Pressing her fist to her solar plexus, she fought down another dry heave. She wasn't weak. She could handle this. She'd seen terrible injuries during her volunteer work at the royal hospital the past few years. But that rash...

She shuddered, something flitting along the edges of her memory, but she quickly pushed it aside. She'd ponder the details of his death later, after they'd left the suite.

Several seconds ticked past. Her heartbeat gradually began to slow. She finally managed to breathe deeply, filling her lungs with Dante's warm, safe, *living* scent.

And suddenly she realized how close they stood—her face nestled into the hollow of his collarbone, his rock-hard thighs pressed against hers. He'd splayed one large hand across the small of her back. His other palm cradled her head.

Her face warming, she leaned back. She didn't even know this man, and she'd wrapped herself around him like bark on a cork tree, ready to climb right into his skin. Loosening the death grip she had on his suit coat, she stepped away and met his gaze. "Sorry."

"You're all right?"

"After seeing that?" Hysteria bubbled inside her. "Not really. I'm going to have nightmares about his eyes for years. But I'm not going to faint, if that's what you mean."

His mouth formed a somber slash. "Yeah, it was bad."

"What do you think happened to him?" A shudder racking her body, she stole a glance at the bathroom door.

"I don't know."

She met his gaze, something in his tone making her wonder if he knew more than he'd let on. But that was silly. What would Dante know about a disease?

Especially that one. She frowned, another sensation of familiarity nagging her at the thought of that awful rash. And then she remembered. She'd recently overheard the doctors at the royal hospital discussing a case....

"We have to go," Dante said, handing over her bag of disks. "We're out of time."

"But I might not have the right disk."

"There was nothing in the bathroom. I looked." Not waiting for an answer, he headed toward the door.

But Paloma didn't move. As anxious as she was to distance herself from Gomez's body, she still needed to find that blackmail evidence. But if it wasn't in the bathroom...

Dante stopped at the door to the suite and frowned back. "What are you doing? We need to go."

"I told you. I can't leave, not until I'm sure I have that disk."

"What difference does it make? Gomez is dead. He can't blackmail you now."

"But the evidence still exists. What if someone else finds it? I have to make sure it's gone for good."

"We don't have time. The power's about to come back on. If we don't go now, the cameras are going to catch us inside."

"But—"

"Listen, Princess. Maybe *you* won't get arrested if they find us here, but I will. And I'll be damned if I'll rot in prison just to cover your royal ass."

The bitterness in his low voice shocked her. Not that she expected him to like her. Few people in País Vell did.

But his anger seemed deeper, almost personal, as if she'd directly caused him harm.

Stung, she crossed her arms. "I'm not doing this for myself."

His gaze sharpened. "No? Then who *are* you doing it for?"

Aware that she'd blundered badly, she rushed to cover the slip. "What I mean is… It's a bad time for this to come out."

That much was true. Three weeks ago, a group of La Brigada separatists had tried to assassinate her family in a bomb blast. Luckily for her, they'd failed. But her father had retaliated hard, imposing a curfew on the separatist region and prohibiting gatherings of any sort. Instead of quelling the rebellion, he'd only angered the separatists further, inciting even more violent protests—which had resulted in several deaths.

She didn't agree with her father's reaction. She'd tried for years to convince him to modernize the monarchy and enact some badly needed reforms—including granting autonomy to Reino Antiguo, which País Vell controlled. But her old-fashioned father refused to change. She had higher hopes for her brother, but Tristan wouldn't assume the throne for years.

In the meantime, it was up to her to protect the citizens of País Vell, even if they thought the worst of her.

"People are already upset with my family," she explained. "If anything bad comes out, they're going to protest again. And someone else could get killed."

He still didn't believe her. Cynicism blazed in his coal-black eyes. But she didn't owe him the truth. They were temporary partners in crime, nothing more.

"Either way, there's nothing else here," he finally said. "It's pointless to hang around."

"I'm not so sure." Still smarting from his derision, she fished the key from the bag and held it out. "I found this in the safe. There must be another one in the suite somewhere."

Dante strode back toward her. He took the key, examined it with the penlight and gave it back. "It doesn't go to a safe. It's the key for a safe-deposit box."

"You mean in a bank? Are you sure?"

He lifted a sardonic brow.

"Right." Of course a thief would recognize keys. But how could she find Gomez's bank box? Where would she even look?

Her panic escalating, she glanced toward the office again. She couldn't leave here without that footage. She'd never have another opportunity to get in. Once the police realized Gomez had died, they would cordon off the area and confiscate his belongings—eliminating any further chance to find clues.

"At least give me a minute to grab his laptop. Maybe he left some information on that."

"Five seconds," Dante warned, his voice hard. "And then you're on your own."

Paloma whirled on her heels and dashed across the penthouse, refusing to dwell on Dante's anger. It didn't matter what he thought. She had far more to worry about than this thief's poor opinion of her. Working quickly, she unplugged the lightweight laptop, tucked it under her arm and raced back across the room.

Dante opened the door to the hall and went out. Her pulse erratic, she trailed him into the vestibule and back to the stairwell door. Then she followed him down the spiral staircase, her mind whirling, her soft boots slapping the stones.

What a disaster. Gomez was dead. She probably

hadn't found the blackmail evidence, so her brother was still at risk. All she had was a bank key, a laptop computer and a handful of random disks which might not yield any clues.

And if anyone discovered she'd been in the penthouse...

She shuddered, picturing the media circus *that* would cause. It would bring back the worst of her scandals, resurrecting the stories of her older brother Felipe's death— which people still blamed on her.

At the bottom of the tower, Dante paused. "We'll head to the service entrance. It's the fastest way out."

"Great." She needed to get past those surveillance cameras before the power came on. Once news of Gomez's death came out, the police would study the footage for signs of foul play—and she couldn't afford to be implicated in any way.

Dante exited the tower. Staying close on his heels, she ran after him down the hallway, trying to decide on a plan. Once she was safely outside the casino, she could circle around to the main entrance and go back in. She would pretend she'd lost sight of her bodyguard when the power went off and feign ignorance about his attack.

But what about the disks and laptop? How was she going to account for them? There was no logical reason for her to have them, no explanation that made sense.

Unless she stowed them in the bushes and returned for them later. But what if someone found them first? She didn't dare risk losing the only possible clue to that blackmail evidence she had.

Tightening her grip on the laptop, she pushed her pace, trying to keep up with Dante's strides. She could ditch her bodyguard completely, pretend she'd hooked up with Dante when the power went out, and have him drive her home. With her wild reputation, no one would question that.

But leaving the casino without her bodyguard would infuriate her father, especially after that assassination attempt. It would reinforce his belief that she was reckless, irresponsible, undoing the efforts she'd made to convince him that she'd reformed.

But what other choice did she have?

Still trying to find a solution, she turned the corner behind Dante and raced down another hall. But suddenly, voices came from the darkness ahead.

"Who's there?" a man called out.

Dante abruptly stopped. Paloma staggered to a halt beside him, a wild spurt of panic robbing her of breath. Now what were they going to do?

"Back here." Dante took hold of her arm and spun her around. But he didn't need to urge her along. She was in an off-limits area of the casino, carrying items stolen from a dead man—in the company of a thief. No way did she want to get caught!

She fled with Dante back down the hallway, running as fast as she could in the dark. But footsteps pounded behind them. "Stop!" the man shouted.

Her pulse frantic, Paloma forced herself to run faster, ignoring the searing burn scorching her lungs. "This way," Dante said, and she veered hard to the left. They entered another hallway, then sprinted full out toward the emergency-exit sign glinting in the darkness a dozen yards ahead.

Almost there. Fatigue weakened her legs. Her breath rasped like a frenzied saw. Calling on all her strength, she sped down the musty hallway, desperate to get outside and disappear into the night, away from prying eyes.

Dante surged ahead. She trained her gaze on the exit sign, still several yards away.

But then a brilliant flash of light filled the air. Blinded by the sudden brightness, Paloma stumbled and nearly fell. Managing to keep hold of the laptop, she pulled herself upright and squinted in the garish light—straight into a surveillance camera mounted beside the door.

Her heart plummeted. They'd just been captured on camera together.

Dante shouldered open the door. Unable to believe that she'd screwed up *yet again,* she barreled after him into the night. Then she staggered to a row of delivery trucks parked beside the loading bay, and stopped.

Her lungs heaved. Her heart beat triple time as she gulped in the crisp night air. She'd messed up, all right. Not only had she failed to find that hidden computer disk, but she'd been recorded on camera with Dante, giving the guards a reason to investigate them.

"Wait here," he said. Before she could ask what he intended, he strode around the truck and disappeared.

Still struggling to breathe normally, she glanced around. Fire trucks rumbled in the parking lot below them. Smoke from the bomb blast lingered in the air, the acrid smell permeating the night. She walked to the end of the alley and scanned the well-heeled people milling around the casino entrance, commenting on the power outage and fire.

Suddenly two guards burst through the emergency exit behind her. Her heart galloping, she moved deeper into the shadows, afraid they would mount a search. But the men just stood on the loading dock for a moment, peering at the commotion outside the casino, then gave up and went inside.

Paloma exhaled. She'd dodged one bullet, at least. But

then the shadows beside her swirled, and she whipped around. "It's me," Dante said, emerging from the darkness.

She pressed her hand to her chest. "You scared me. I thought you were a guard."

"Sorry." He stepped closer, moving into a circle of light, and she caught the tension lines bracketing his mouth.

Her belly tightened again. "What happened?"

"I'll tell you later. Let's get out of here first. My car's at the edge of the lot."

Not seeing an alternative, she fell in beside him, but her anxiety ratcheted up a notch as they went across the lot. Something had put that worry in his eyes, but what?

Still mulling that over, she wove behind him through the rows of parked cars. People streamed around them, chattering about the night's events. Paloma ducked her head, hoping no one recognized her—a complication she didn't need.

Dante stopped beside a dinged-up hatchback. "Get in. It's not locked."

Surprised at his choice of cars, she climbed inside. While she buckled her seat belt, Dante grabbed a knapsack from beneath a nearby shrub and tossed it into the back. Then he slid into the driver's seat and fiddled with some loose wires under the dash.

She blinked. "You stole this car?"

"I was trying to stay anonymous." He shot her a pointed look. "A lot of good that did."

She dragged her gaze to the windshield as the old car stuttered to life. She'd definitely fouled up. Getting caught on camera with Dante would create exactly the kind of publicity she'd hoped to avoid—and put innocent people at risk.

Including him.

Although *innocent* hardly described Dante Quevedo. She cast a glance at his profile as he drove through the gravel lot. She skimmed his dark, stubbled jaw, his big hands grasping the wheel, the heavy bones of his wrists. And that restless feeling quivered through her, that primitive, carnal awareness he'd evoked in her from the start.

Determined to ignore it, she turned her gaze to the blackened forest as they left the grounds of the casino and whizzed down the mountain road. Dante disturbed her, all right. And she never should have enlisted his help. Now he was mired with her in this muddled mess— and it was up to her to get them out.

He shifted to a lower gear. The car slowed abruptly, jerking her against the seat belt, the engine protesting with a high-pitched shriek. He hit the brakes, slowing them even further, and steered the car off the road. The beams from the headlights bounced across the trees as they bumped over the rocky ground.

"What are you doing?" She braced her hand against the dashboard as the car lurched through a rocky ditch. "Why did you leave the road?"

"They've set up a roadblock closer to town."

"How do you know that?"

"I overheard some people talking in the parking lot."

She frowned. "You think they know that Gomez is dead?"

"No. They're looking for you. Your bodyguard got a good look at me before the lights went out. When he woke up and couldn't find you, he probably figured I'd kidnapped you."

Oh, God. Dante was right. That was exactly what

Carlos would think. She sank back against the seat, fastening her gaze on the passing timber as the implications sank in. Her father would act at once. He'd scour the countryside, mobilizing the military and mounting an all-out search.

Her forehead suddenly throbbing, she pressed her fingers to her temples and tried to think. "I'll straighten this out as soon as I get home. I'll call my father and let him know that I'm all right."

"He's not going to believe you."

"Why not?"

Dante swerved again. "They saw us together in the hall, and we were running away from the guards. How are you going to explain that?"

"I'll say I was lost, that you were helping me find my way out. And we ran because…because we didn't know who they were. We thought the guards were someone else, maybe La Brigada raiding the casino. And you were trying to keep me safe."

"It still won't work."

"Of course it will. Once I explain—"

"I'm a thief, Paloma. I've got a criminal record. It won't matter what you say. They'll assume that I coerced you and throw me back in jail."

"Not without proof, they won't."

"Proof?" He shot her an incredulous look. "What planet do you live on? Since when do they need proof to arrest someone?"

"That's awfully cynical. Our laws—"

He barked out a bitter laugh. "Laws. Right. That's why they tossed me in jail before—with no lawyer, no contact with the outside world, no chance to fight the charges, whatever the hell they were."

"I don't believe that."

"Then you're either stupid or naive."

She frowned at his angry profile, his bitterness bothering her. True, she hadn't found his arrest papers. And she knew the system wasn't perfect, that some of the older guards were corrupt. But Dante made the country sound medieval. And while her father might be high-handed, he'd never tolerate abuses like that.

"I don't know what happened with your arrest," she admitted. "So I can't argue with you about that. But you don't have to worry about tonight. I'll make sure my father knows that you didn't do anything wrong. I'll talk to him in person and prove that I'm all right."

Dante slanted her a glance. "There's still one problem."

"What?"

"*I* don't believe *you*."

The car hit a rut, and she clutched the seat. He didn't believe she'd stand up for him? "Why not?"

"Why should I?"

"Because I said I would. And my word is good."

"Your word?" he scoffed. "You've been lying to me from the start. There isn't a chance in hell Gomez was blackmailing you with the reputation you have."

She flushed and crossed her arms, unable to deny the truth. "The reason I need that disk doesn't matter."

"It matters. I'm in this mess as much as you are, so you damned well owe me the truth. And until I get it, I'm not letting you out of my sight."

"What?"

"You heard me, Princess. You're stuck with me until I decide we're through."

Outraged, she clamped her jaw. Then she turned her gaze to the side window, where the wind whistled through a crack. *Wonderful.* She'd thought the night couldn't get much worse. But she'd been wrong.

Because now she had to worry about *him.*

Chapter 3

Dante had to hand it to the princess. She'd lived up to
her bad reputation and totally screwed up his night.

Furious over the debacle she'd landed him in, he
stopped on a cobblestone street in the heart of the ancient city and parked. Darkness enveloped the car. A dog
barked from a nearby house, its sharp, high-pitched yaps
adding to his foul mood.

Paloma had embroiled him in a disaster, all right. The
police were hot on his trail. They would assume he'd abducted the princess and would probably shoot him on
sight. They'd definitely connect him to that bomb blast—
and possibly the casino owner's bizarre death.

And until he could extricate himself from this unholy
mess, he wasn't letting her escape. She was the only hope
he had to clear his name and keep himself out of jail.

"Where are we?" she asked.

He turned his head, barely able to make out her features in the predawn light. She hadn't spoken for the last half hour as they'd worked their way down the forest trail. She'd sat with her arms folded tight, her sultry lips compressed, upset that he didn't trust her, no doubt. Well, too damned bad. He needed answers. And he intended to get them, even if her feelings got hurt.

"A property I'm restoring," he hedged. "No one will find us there. We can talk, make plans." *Figure out what had gone wrong.*

Still seething over his predicament, he climbed out, grabbed his knapsack from the backseat and did a visual check of the car, making sure he hadn't left incriminating evidence behind. Then he led the way up the cobbled lane into the oldest part of the city, a once-lavish section that bordered the fortified wall.

The barking abruptly stopped. The cold wind gusted in the sudden silence, sending a plastic bag skittering over the stones. Dante glanced at Paloma walking beside him, the light from a wrought-iron lantern casting a silver sheen over her hair.

She hadn't set out to harm him; he'd give her that much. His friend Rafael Navarro never would have agreed to help her if she had. And given her reaction to Gomez's corpse, she also hadn't expected to find the casino owner dead.

But her blackmail story still stank. Why would anyone threaten to expose her with the wild reputation she had? Unless she really was protecting someone else...

Dante slid her a speculative look. She stared straight ahead, her profile blurred by shadows, her long hair fluttering in the breeze. Who else could she be shielding? Her father? Her brother? Anticipation roared through him at the thought. If she was protecting her brother, that blackmail evidence could be the proof he needed to finally destroy that bloody murderer—hell, the entire royal family—including the spoiled princess at his side.

His conscience twinged, but he beat back any qualms. *No mercy.* The nobles sure hadn't shown any to the hapless people of País Vell. For centuries, a few powerful families had controlled the country's wealth while the impoverished masses struggled to survive—scrabbling for medical care and food, working to put a decent roof over their heads.

And anyone who dared protest was mowed down in a hail of bullets—like his desperate mother, shot point-blank while her two terrified children looked on.

Dante steeled his jaw, beating back the fury, knowing he had to keep his agenda under wraps. Because no matter how innocuous Paloma seemed, she was a royal, his sworn enemy. And he couldn't risk tipping her off.

He reached the medieval stone cross that had once marked a pilgrim trail and turned down the cobbled lane. Halfway down the block, he reached a thick wooden door in the high stone wall and stopped.

Paloma came to a halt beside him, then peered up at the escutcheon above the door. "This is the Palacio de los Arcos." Named after the impressive arches that lined the courtyard inside.

"Yeah, so?"

She turned her gaze to his. "This used to be in my family. I came here a few times when my great-aunt Pilar was still alive. I tried to convince my father to buy it after she died, but he said it needed too much work."

"It was a mess, all right." So bad, in fact, that he'd bought the condemned estate for next to nothing, barely more than the price of the lot. But what he'd saved on price he'd paid for in labor. It had taken him a year just to stabilize the building and keep it from collapsing.

"And you're doing the restoration?" she asked.

He'd bought the property under a sham corporation so the police couldn't connect it to him—but he wasn't about to tell her that. "That's right."

He swung up the iron knocker, tapped a code on the hidden keypad, then pulled open the heavy door.

"That's clever the way you hid that," she said.

"I didn't want to ruin the look of the door." He stood back to let her through.

She stepped inside, her subtle floral scent twining around him like a lover's embrace. Disgusted that he'd noticed, he followed her into the courtyard, but the swing of her slender hips, the thick mass of chestnut hair tumbling down her back accelerated his pulse.

He clenched his jaw. No way. He wasn't going down that futile track. She wasn't his date. She was a means to an end, nothing more.

She stopped beside the fountain, then slowly turned around, gazing up at the three-tiered gallery of arches towering on every side. In its heyday, the once magnificent palace had hosted a variety of foreign dignitaries, including the monarchs of France and Spain.

Which perfectly illustrated the chasm between their lives.

"Oh, wow," she breathed. "You've done all this work?"

"Yeah." Bit by bit, in between his charity heists and legitimate stonemasonry jobs. And he still had a long way to go. He scanned the boards piled against one wall, the scaffolding stretched across the courtyard, the mountain of paint cans and saws.

"It's beautiful," she breathed. "I love the way you've preserved the original features. It's modern, but still antique."

He met her gaze, impressed that she understood. "That was the point."

"Well, it worked. It's really lovely, just amazing. You do fabulous work."

Despite his resolve to keep his distance, her frank admiration burrowed beneath his defenses and evoked a glimmer of pride. He'd spent years working on the sixteenth-century palace, staining the chestnut beams, piecing together the damaged frescoes, painstakingly repairing the terra-cotta tiles. Shoring up the dilapidated, graffiti-marred structure to create a home for his baby sister and fill the void in her troubled life.

But Paloma wouldn't understand that. She'd been raised in an opulent castle, surrounded by every luxury, worlds apart from his hardscrabble upbringing, where he'd had to steal to survive.

"This way," he said, hardening his voice. He strode into one of the few rooms he'd finished and snapped on a high-powered lamp. The harsh light flooded the room, banishing the feeling of intimacy she'd sparked. Still clutching the laptop and bag of disks, Paloma sank onto the leather sofa and glanced around the room. He settled in the opposite chair.

For a minute, he simply watched her, studying her full, pouty lips, the sooty lashes rimming her hypnotic eyes, the shimmering fall of her chestnut hair. Her undeniable beauty washed through him, the feminine lines of her face, the creamy glow of her skin jump-starting his heart. Had she been anyone else...

But she wasn't anyone else. She was Paloma Vergara, the princess. A member of the family he planned to destroy.

He braced his forearms on his knees. "All right. Let's

take this from the top. What were you after back there? And I want the truth this time."

She hesitated, her apparent unwillingness to confide in him irritating him even more. "Look, Princess. Thanks to you, I've got the royal guards gunning for me. If I'm going to get arrested, I deserve to know what for."

She pushed her hands through her hair, the honeyed highlights shimmering like gold in the light. Her weary sigh filled the air. "You're right. It's my fault you're in this mess. But I really did tell you the truth—most of it, at least. I'm looking for blackmail evidence."

He cocked a brow. "And?"

Setting aside the bag and laptop, she rose. She paced to the still-dark windows, then turned and faced him again. "What I'm about to tell you... You can't tell anyone. You have to promise. Because if the media finds out..."

"Forget it. I'm not promising anything. Not until I know what this is about."

"But—"

"I said to forget it." He stood and stalked toward her, stopping so close beside her she had to tilt back her head to meet his eyes. "I agreed to get you into that penthouse, and I did my part. Now it's time that you came clean."

Her lush mouth flattened, her eyes flashing with annoyance at his hard line. But after several tense seconds, she released her breath. "All right. The truth is... It wasn't me Gomez was blackmailing. It was my brother, Tristan."

Dante's gut stilled. Excitement leaped inside him, sending adrenaline surging into his veins. He'd guessed right. And this was exactly what he needed—information that could incriminate the prince.

"He gambles," she continued with a little shrug.

"Nothing major. He's not addicted or anything. He just goes to the casino a couple times a month. It's not a secret."

"I've heard that." According to his sister, who'd worked as a waitress at the casino, the prince gambled regularly in the high-roller rooms. "So what happened?"

"The last time he was there, he gambled with a man he'd never met before. Someone from the Middle East. He didn't think much of it at the time. But he found out later that the man was a terrorist, a member of the Third Crescent, an al Qaeda offshoot. And apparently the surveillance camera caught them together."

"So? What's wrong with that? If he didn't know who the man was…"

"You're right. Normally no one would care. But my father just signed an international agreement, promising cooperation in the war on terror. Tristan's heading the committee in charge of that, so pictures of him partying with a terrorist…" She grimaced. "The timing couldn't be worse. It would make us look corrupt, especially with the reputation for smuggling that País Vell has.

"And you know what the mood in the country is like. People are angry at my family right now. Any hint of scandal will only add to the unrest. And if people start protesting again, someone else could get hurt."

Dante rubbed his jaw, his morning beard stubble scraping his palm. "Even so, just gambling with a terrorist doesn't seem that bad. It's hardly worthy of blackmail."

"It will be by the time the tabloids get finished with it. They'll distort and exaggerate the story until Tristan looks like a terrorist, too. Just the appearance of doing something wrong is enough. Believe me, I've learned that the hard way over the years."

He angled his head, her obvious resentment taking him aback. And for the first time he wondered if he'd misjudged her, and if there was more to her than he knew. Because if the tabloids had exaggerated her behavior, painting her in an unfair light...

Shocked by the direction of his thoughts, he cut them off. He didn't care what she was like. She was a tool, a means to avenge his sister's death, nothing more.

"So Gomez tried to blackmail your brother?" he prodded, steering his thoughts back to the prince.

"Yes. He told Tristan to pay up, or he'd expose the surveillance footage."

"And when was this?"

"The gambling trip? A couple of weeks ago, on a Thursday night."

Dante's heart missed several beats. It took every ounce of effort he had to keep his expression blank. His sister had died that night. And there wasn't a chance in hell it was a coincidence, not with the prince involved. Whatever had happened in the casino *had* to be connected to her death.

His excitement rising, he paced across the tiles. Lucía had worked the late shift at the casino that night. Just after her shift had ended, she'd phoned him in a panic, her voice so slurred and incoherent, and hiccupping so badly, he could hardly make sense of her words. She'd claimed that the prince was trying to kill her, that she'd witnessed something dreadful—something involving shootings or shots.

Of course, that last part didn't make sense. She hadn't suffered a gunshot wound—only a needle mark on her arm. The coroner had ruled her death a massive heroin overdose, which Dante refused to believe.

But assuming the prince had killed her, the question

was *why?* She might have seen him gambling with the terrorist—but what difference would that have made? She wouldn't have recognized anyone from the Middle East.

Unless the "shots" referred to a murder. If the prince had killed someone—maybe the terrorist—and Lucía had witnessed the crime, he'd have a motive to shut her up.

But then what about Gomez? How did his death figure into this? What was that weird-looking rash about?

Dante stopped by the entrance to the kitchen and turned around, his gaze traveling to Paloma again. She still stood by the window, her full lips pursed, her wary eyes on his. He didn't know who or what had killed Gomez, but he did know one thing. Whatever had happened to his sister that night, that blackmail evidence *had* to hold the key.

Knowing he had to be careful, that one wrong move could make Paloma suspicious of him and destroy his plans, he walked back to where she stood. "So how did you get involved in this?"

She scooped her hair over one shoulder and twisted the ends. "Tristan came to me for advice. He needed to confide in someone he could trust."

"But why have *you* look for the evidence?" he asked, pressing. "You're not a thief. And what if you got caught? Wouldn't that cause a scandal, too?"

She lifted one slender shoulder in a shrug. "Yes, but not as much. It would still make the people angry, but my reputation's already bad—as you pointed out. No one expects better from me. But Tristan's going to be king some day. He can't afford a scandal that big."

Dante crossed his arms, her willingness to sacrifice herself for her brother ticking him off. Loyalty he understood. But that scumbag prince didn't deserve a break. "You weren't the one partying with a terrorist. You shouldn't have to pay the price."

She flushed. "You don't understand. Tristan's young. He's made mistakes, but he'll make a good leader some day. And he's always depended on me. He's six years younger than I am. And I guess...I feel more like a mother than a sister to him sometimes."

He mulled that over, adding it to what he knew of her family's past. He knew that the queen had died in child-birth. That Paloma's older brother—the original heir to the throne—had died in a hiking accident when they were kids, an accident rumored to be Paloma's fault. That the king was an alcoholic who spent his evenings drowning his bitterness in a bottle—when he wasn't repressing the unlucky citizens of País Vell.

Dante had never sympathized with the royals. He'd been too busy struggling through his own life to care about theirs—too busy burying his murdered mother. Too busy raising his fragile sister and trying to keep her off drugs. Too busy helping the impoverished people of País Vell survive their precarious lives.

"Haven't you ever felt that way?" Paloma asked. "Isn't there someone you want to protect?"

"Yeah," he admitted. "My sister, Lucía."

"She's younger than you are?"

His jaw turned stiff. "She *was* younger. Now she's dead."

Paloma's startled eyes shot to his. "I'm sorry. I didn't... I know how hard that is."

Did she? Skeptical, he held her gaze, wondering if the compassion in her eyes was real. Maybe she did understand. Maybe she felt responsible for her older brother's death. But he didn't want her sympathy. He didn't want to feel any connection to her.

And he never should have mentioned Lucía. The wound was still too fresh, his guilt over his failure to protect her still gnawing at him, day and night.

"But you can see, then, why I needed to help?" she asked softly.

"Yeah. I understand." And that was exactly why he was here. He'd failed Lucía once. He refused to do it again. He had to avenge her killing, no matter what it took.

But one thing was clear. He had to be careful. Paloma had just admitted that she'd do anything to protect her brother, even sacrifice her reputation on his behalf. If she suspected that Dante intended to harm him, she'd make sure he ended up behind bars.

Trying to figure out the best way to play this, he crossed the room to his chair. A second later, Paloma returned to the sofa and sat.

He cleared his throat. "Look, I know you don't want me involved in this—"

"There's really no need. You've already done your part."

"I don't have much choice now that I've been caught on camera with you."

A flush climbed up her cheeks. "That's my fault. If I hadn't taken the time to get that laptop…" She shook her head, making her hair spill over her arms. "I promise I'll talk to my father. I'll straighten everything out. And I swear I'll make sure that you aren't blamed. You really can trust me on that."

He frowned. He couldn't force her to stay with him. He needed her cooperation if he hoped to get information from her.

"I have a better idea. Maybe we can work together to find that surveillance footage you need."

She stilled, suddenly alert. "Why? What would you get out of this?"

He picked his words, not wanting to arouse her suspicions and tip her off. "I told you my sister died. But I didn't tell you where. She died at the casino a couple of weeks ago."

"What? How?"

"A heroin overdose. At least that's what the coroner said."

"You don't agree?"

He shook his head. "She'd been clean for months. And her drug of choice was oxycodone. She got addicted years ago when she hurt her back."

Paloma hesitated. "I know you don't want to think it, but is there a chance you might be wrong? It wouldn't be the first time an addict lied."

"I know." Lucía had fallen off the wagon often enough for him to know. "But it's not just that. You remember Gomez's rash?"

She shuddered. "I'm hardly likely to forget it."

"I found my sister's body in the parking lot. She looked… She had a similar rash."

Paloma's head came up. "You're saying she had the same thing as Gomez?"

"I don't know." His sister had claimed the prince was trying to kill her, which would rule out any disease. "But I need to find out. If you help me find out what really killed her, I'll help you look for what you need."

"But if they both had a disease…" Horror filled her eyes. "Oh, God. What if it's contagious? What if we got exposed?"

"All the more reason to work together. We both have

a stake in this now." He leaned forward and extended his hand. "So what do you say? Do we have a deal?"

"I don't know." She scrubbed her face with her hands, then sighed. "Yes. All right. It's a deal."

"Good." His hand closed over hers. The soft feel of her skin jolted through him, electrifying his pulse. And a sudden sliver of warning crept through his mind.

He had to be careful. Paloma was dangerous. There was something different about this woman, something about her that threatened to creep beneath his defenses....

No mercy, he reminded himself firmly.

But he'd better keep his wits about him if he hoped to survive.

Chapter 4

Paloma tugged back her hand, the startling warmth of Dante's skin, the rough, calloused feel of his palm igniting a sudden flurry of excitement inside her and scattering her pulse.

Heat scalded her cheeks. She crossed her arms, trying to cover up her response. What in heaven's name was wrong with her? All he'd done was shake her hand, and her senses had run amok.

She had no business responding to him like that. So what if he was hot—gorgeous in a rough-hewn, masculine way? He was a thief, possibly even the infamous Fantasma, the worst possible person for her.

And he didn't even like her. She snuck a glance at his craggy profile as he lifted the laptop off the floor. She hadn't missed the disdain in his icy eyes, or how his mouth curled down when he looked her way. He clearly wasn't her fan.

Which was fine. Dante's bad opinion of her didn't matter, even if he did make her senses hum. She had far more important things on her mind—that blackmail evidence. Gomez's death. That dreadful rash.

Her mind swerving back to Dante's bombshell, she hugged her arms even tighter as she struggled to process the news. "If Gomez did have a disease, we need to let the authorities know. Someone else could be at risk."

Dante straightened and met her gaze, his eyes more guarded now. "Let's look at his computer first and find out if we have the evidence you need. Then we can worry about how he died."

That made sense. The blackmail evidence took priority as the more immediate threat to the stability of País Vell. Besides, until they knew exactly what had killed Gomez, they couldn't risk starting rumors. They needed more information first.

Dante led the way into the kitchen. He flicked on an overhead light switch, then headed to a farmhouse table at the edge of the spacious room. Paloma paused in the doorway, her gaze traveling over the polished tile floor, the high, vaulted ceiling with chestnut beams, a fireplace big enough to stand in along one wall. Once again, Dante had preserved the original structure while accommodating modern tastes. He'd knocked down some walls, creating a modern, airy kitchen in what had once been a servants' galley with little charm or light.

And that was the problem, she decided as she joined him at the table and sat. This man fascinated her on so many levels—from his unconventional, criminal lifestyle to his incredible attention to detail in his restoration work, to the pain in his eyes when he'd spoken of his sister's death.

He hooked a chair with his foot, dragged it closer to

hers, and sat. Then he turned on the laptop, angling it so they both could see.

She skimmed the sexy quirk of his lips, the impressive definition in his arms. He had heavy, corded forearms, biceps that looked sculpted from steel. But of course, he'd have muscles. He spent his days chiseling and hauling stones.

"You still have that key?" he asked.

Realizing she was ogling him again, she emptied the bag of disks on the table, picked up the tiny envelope and handed it to him. He shook out the key and held it up to the light, his dark eyes intent.

"What do you think?" she asked.

"There's nothing on it, but that's not unusual. Banks normally don't mark their keys. It's too easy for them to get lost." He nodded toward the laptop. "Mind if I look at his files?"

"What do you think you'll find?"

"Bank records, hopefully. They should show a monthly charge for a safe-deposit box."

That made sense. "Go ahead."

He set down the key and pulled the laptop closer, the light from the screen carving hollows beneath his cheeks. She dragged her gaze to the computer, determined not to let her attention stray as he flipped through the various files.

"No luck?" she asked a minute later.

"Nothing obvious. I'll check his directory for hidden files." His fingers flew over the keyboard, and then he paused. "Here's something. *Finances.* This could be it."

Paloma leaned closer, anticipation rippling through her as he double clicked on the file. "What if he uses more than one bank?" she asked.

"He might. But I doubt he has more than one safe-deposit box."

The screen flickered and changed. A message box appeared, containing a log-in space.

Her heart sank. "We need his password." The way her luck was running, she shouldn't have been surprised. "I suppose there's no way around it."

"Not really." Dante minimized the page, then continued clicking on files. After a minute he sat back. "It's not here. I thought he might have a vault for his passwords, but he's not that high-tech. He probably keeps them on a piece of paper in his desk."

She glanced at him in alarm. "You're not thinking of going back there?" They couldn't risk getting caught.

"You have a better idea?"

She leaned back in her chair and tried to think. There was no point in phoning the banks and asking if Gomez had an account. No reputable financial institution would give that information out. Besides, Gomez might not have banked in País Vell. There were hundreds of banks in the surrounding European countries—far too many to search.

"We need to find someone who can get around that password," she decided. But who? She didn't dare involve her father's security team in this. If he caught wind of the blackmail scheme, he'd be furious.

"I have a friend who can probably help," Dante said. "A computer hacker I know. He's the one who cut the power to the casino so we could get in."

"I thought you did that."

"I only disabled the backup generators. Miguel did the rest."

She rolled that over in her mind. "You're sure we can trust him?"

"He came through for us at the casino. Rafe can vouch for him, too."

She creased her brow, hating to rely on someone she didn't know. But Rafael Navarro was the fiancé of her old school friend, Gabrielle Ferrer. And Paloma knew their judgment was sound. Besides, Dante had as much at stake as she did, maybe more. He'd hardly recommend a man they couldn't trust.

"All right. Go ahead and ask him to help."

"I'll call him right now." Dante tugged his cell phone from his back pocket. He punched in a number, then rose and headed toward the sink. "Coffee?" he called back.

"Sure." Her gaze went to the laptop again. "I'll check the rest of these disks, then start looking for information about that rash."

Dante turned on the faucet to fill the coffee machine, and the running water muffled his voice. Shifting her mind to Gomez, Paloma made short work of the disks and flash drives, which contained only his correspondence from the past few years.

Hoping she'd have better luck identifying what killed him, she opened a search engine on the computer and typed in the keyword *rash*. Several pages later she'd seen images of everything from shingles and smallpox to rosacea, but nothing that even remotely resembled Gomez's horrific face.

She added the word *diseases*. Still nothing. She sat back and frowned at the screen.

"Miguel's going to meet us at the Roman bridge in an hour," Dante said from the kitchen island. "He wants to take the laptop back to his place. You have a problem with that?"

Paloma rose and walked to the island. She hated to give up control of the laptop. It was the only possible link to that blackmail evidence she had. But she couldn't do this alone. And the longer it took to find that surveillance footage, the greater the chance that something else would go wrong.

"As long as you're sure we can trust this guy."

Dante set two cups of coffee on the counter, and his gaze connected with hers. "I told you we can."

"It's just…I've been burned before." She added sugar to her coffee and stirred it in. "When you're a public figure like I am, you never know when someone's going to leak something to the tabloids to make a buck. It doesn't even matter if it's true."

He cocked his head. "You're saying the stories they've published about you aren't true?"

Wishing she could claim just that, she sighed. "No. Most of them are true. Exaggerated, maybe, but I've made my share of mistakes. I haven't exactly been a saint."

His dark eyes warmed. The corners of his mouth kicked up in a wickedly carnal smile that brought a rush of heat to her loins. Then he lowered his gaze, forging a slow, hot path to her breasts and back, and her heart did somersaults in her chest.

"I never did care for saints," he said, his voice even huskier now.

Her pulse skittered and lurched. She lifted her cup and gulped down some coffee, counting on the quick jolt of caffeine to bring her back to earth. But her knees felt weak, every nerve ending sizzling with sensual awareness. Dante was hard enough to resist when he acted surly. But when he turned on the charm, leveling that bad-boy smile her way…

"Any luck finding that rash?" he asked, suddenly all business again.

She took another sip of the espresso coffee, needing time to compose herself. "Not so far. None of the images even come close."

Forcing her mind back to Gomez, she carried her cup to the table and sat. After fortifying herself with another sip of the strong coffee, she continued her search, entering more keywords.

So Dante had flirted a bit. So he'd exhibited some typical male interest and checked her out. It didn't mean anything. He was hardly going to hit on her after the hostility he'd shown all night.

"Try searching for bleeding," he suggested, lowering himself into his chair.

"All right." Conscious of his rock-hard thigh just inches from hers, she typed in *bleeding disease*. "Hemophilia, von Willebrand disease. That's not right."

Next she tried *bleeding red eyes*. "Trauma, broken blood vessels," she read, skimming down the links. "Nosebleeds. That's ridiculous." Gomez hadn't died of anything as simple as a nosebleed. He'd bled everywhere, profusely, spreading copious pools of blood over the tiled floor.

Shuddering at the memory, she entered *profuse bleeding,* but still nothing pertinent came up. Growing frustrated, she added *death*.

The page flickered again. A dozen links came up, and she skimmed the words. "Dengue fever. An epidemic in Yemen, possibly caused by sarin gas. Pregnant women in India dying from contaminated IVs. Hemorrhagic fever…"

Her heart skipped a beat. She slid her gaze down the list. Marburg. Lassa.

Ebola Zaire.

"Oh, God," she whispered, appalled. She gave Dante a horrified look. "That can't be it."

"What?"

"Ebola. Hemorrhagic fever." Stunned, she clicked on a link. A map of Africa appeared on the screen. "It occurs mostly in Africa. Zaire, Sudan. Not Europe." Certainly not País Vell. Unless Gomez had traveled recently...

But no, it had to be something else. At least she prayed it was. Even the thought of Ebola terrified her. Hardly anyone who contracted it survived.

"Are there any pictures?" Dante asked.

"I'll see." She clicked on another link and slowly scrolled down the page. "It incubates for two to twenty-one days," she read. "The symptoms are fever, sore throat, weakness, diarrhea, cough. Did your sister have any of those?"

"No. Not at all. And she sure as hell didn't travel to the Sudan."

Paloma eased out a shaky breath. "Then it has to be something else." *Thank God.* She scrolled down the page even farther. "It leads to a rash, red eyes and hiccups, of all the odd things. Death occurs in the second week."

She glanced at him. His face had paled, and his mouth had turned suddenly grim.

"What is it?" she asked. "Did your sister—"

"Just keep looking."

"But—"

"She was fine when she went to work that night."

Her nerves wound tight. "So it couldn't be that. She would have had symptoms, right? The disease would have to incubate for a while. She wouldn't just suddenly get sick and die."

But what if it *was* Ebola? What if Gomez had caught

it from Dante's sister? And what about that patient at the hospital? Could his symptoms have been the same?

"There was a case at the hospital where I volunteer, a man who died recently with a strange rash. It was just about a week ago, in fact."

Dante's gaze sharpened on hers. "He looked like Gomez?"

"I don't know. I never saw him. I just overheard one of the doctors discussing the case." She pressed her hand to her belly, apprehension making her ill. "They called the coroner in. He was going to send the tissue samples to a lab in Spain. They probably have the results by now."

"If it's Ebola, what would they do?"

"Notify the health authorities. Issue an alert. Maybe quarantine people. It's highly contagious. Ninety percent of the people who get it die."

And she'd stood beside Gomez in the bathroom, breathing the air. She'd taken her gloves off, then touched the counter, the faucet, the door....

Her lungs closed up. A wild feeling of panic drained her of any warmth. She had to be wrong. How would Ebola have arrived in País Vell?

"We can't tell anyone yet," she told Dante. "Not until we're sure. People would go crazy." There'd be a mass stampede from the country, a rush on the pharmacies for drugs, total panic in the streets....

"So what do you want to do?" Dante asked.

"We need more information. But Dr. Sanz, the doctor who treated that patient works the late shift. He won't be in until this afternoon."

"Can you get his home phone number?"

"Not easily." Not without raising questions. "But we could talk to the coroner while we wait. He conducted the autopsy." Dante grimaced, and she raised her brows. "What? You don't want to talk to him?"

"What's the point? The guy's a quack. He's the one who claimed my sister overdosed."

Not wanting to hurt his feelings, she chose her words carefully. "And you're sure that's not true?"

He tipped back in his chair and crossed his arms. "She swore she'd gone straight."

"Addicts have been known to lie."

"I know that, but she really had changed her life. She was holding down her waitressing job and staying away from her old friends."

He believed he'd failed her. Her heart wobbled at the sudden insight, the guilt in his voice striking a chord. She understood that guilt. She'd failed to save her older brother Felipe's life. And she'd lived with the pain of that failure every day for fifteen years.

"It still seems odd that the coroner could have made a mistake like that," she said. "How could he have confused a disease with a drug overdose?"

"She had a needle mark on her arm," Dante admitted. "He said she had other signs, too—like her blue lips and discolored tongue."

Paloma chewed her lip. A needle mark sounded damning to her. "But if she slipped and took some oxycodone...maybe there was heroin mixed with it—or some other kind of drug. And maybe it caused her to look like that."

Dante shook his head. "I told you, she'd gone straight."

"Then you're probably right," she said, knowing it was futile to argue that now. "The coroner made a mistake. Either way, he should have the lab results by now. We can ask for a copy and see for ourselves."

"I guess." Dante straightened his chair with a thud. "If you think it will help, give him a call."

She glanced at the still-dark window above the sink. "It's too early. He won't be in his office yet. Why don't we stop by there after we drop the laptop off?"

"All right." Dante shrugged off his suit jacket and stood. The stark white fabric of his dress shirt drew her gaze to his tawny skin. Suddenly feeling breathless, she looked away.

"I'm going to change clothes," he continued. "There's a bathroom down the hall. Help yourself to anything you want in the fridge."

Paloma blinked as he strode off. Was this *his* house? He'd just insinuated as much. But why hadn't he admitted that from the start? Unless he routinely kept a change of clothes at his work sites…

Mulling that over, she gathered their dirty cups and washed them in the sink. Was she being naive to trust him? Could Dante have some hidden motive for offering to help her out? But that was nuts. She'd thought up this plan. She'd arranged for his release from jail. And naturally he'd want to work together when they'd both been caught on camera.

Deciding the long, stressful night had clouded her thinking, she turned off the tap and dried her hands. Her gaze landed on his cell phone, which he'd left beside the sink. No matter what secrets he had, she'd promised to clear his name. And since Tristan had precipitated this disaster, it was time her brother did his part to get them out.

He answered on the second ring.

"Tristan, it's me, Paloma."

"Where the hell have you been?" His voice exploded over the line. "I've been waiting for you all night. Carlos called with some lamebrained story that you'd been kidnapped. Did you get that computer disk?"

"I'm fine," she said, annoyed that he hadn't bothered to ask. But of course, he was frantic about the blackmail. She had to cut him some slack. "And no, I didn't get it. It wasn't there."

He let out a stream of obscenities.

Wincing, she held the phone from her ear. "Calm down," she told him when he paused to take a breath. "I'll have it soon. We think he hid it in a safe-deposit box, so we're trying to find the bank."

"We?" Tristan's voice rose. "What do you mean *we?* Who else is involved in this?"

"Just someone who helped me get into the penthouse. But don't worry," she said when he started to swear again. "We can trust him. He's not going to leak this to the media."

"You mean like Rick Castro?"

Her face burned at that low blow. She'd dated that slime bag briefly—until he'd posted the nude photos he'd taken with a hidden camera on the internet. "Thanks for reminding me."

Tristan paused. "Sorry. I probably shouldn't have made that crack. But you don't have the best track record when it comes to men. And I can't afford to have this come out."

Irritated, she rubbed the dull ache forming between her brows. "You think I can? I'm the one who broke into the casino. The media will go nuts if they find out."

"I know, I know. We both need to get that evidence fast." His voice turned placating now. "So who is this guy who's helping you?"

"A thief I hired. His name doesn't matter. But he didn't kidnap me," she said, warding off another protest. "So tell Father to call off the guards. If they interfere in this, I'll never find it in time."

Tristan didn't answer.

"Did you hear me?" she asked. "I need you to talk to him."

"Yeah, I heard you. I'll talk to him as soon as he gets up. So where are you now?"

"Somewhere safe. Don't worry about that," she said when he tried to cut in. "But there's something else you need to know. César Gomez is dead."

Silence fell. "Dead?" Tristan finally asked, sounding stunned. "You killed him?"

"Of course not!"

"Then who did?"

"No one, I don't think. It looked as if he died of some disease." She shivered at the memory of his bloated corpse. "It was really awful. All that blood..."

Another long silence filled the line.

Trying not to envision Gomez, she dragged in a steadying breath. "Listen, Tristan. We need to find out what happened to him. If this is a disease, it could spread. You need to be ready to take action, just in case. We'll have to inform the health authorities and implement our emergency plan. Don't do it yet, but make sure you're prepared.

"And keep people away from that penthouse for a while. But don't tell them why. I don't want anyone to know that we've been inside."

"What are you going to do?" Tristan asked.

"Talk to the coroner as soon as his office opens."

"But if he doesn't know about Gomez—"

"It's complicated. We think there might have been another case or two, but I'll explain that later on."

Tristan fell silent again. "What about the disk?" he finally asked.

"I told you, I've got that under control." She heard the thud of approaching footsteps and cupped her hand over the phone. "I've got to go. I'll call you as soon as I find something out."

"But—"

She hung up and set down the phone, a sudden spurt of guilt bringing a rush of warmth to her face. But that was silly. She didn't have anything to hide. Tristan had a right to know the status of that blackmail evidence.

Then Dante strolled into the kitchen, looking like the ultimate bad boy with two motorcycle helmets tucked under his arm. His gaze stalled on hers, and awareness quivered through her, rattling her nerves.

And before she could stop it, her gaze traveled over his impossibly broad shoulders to his flat, sexy abdomen and the bulge in his faded jeans. He hadn't shaved, and the dark scruff covering his jaw added to the carnal look.

Her throat went dry, his blatant masculinity wreaking havoc on her pulse. And she knew with a bone-deep certainty that she had to watch her step. This man was trouble. He had secrets. She'd be a fool to give him her trust.

But as he stalked across the kitchen toward her, his coal-black eyes making her stomach flip, she knew she faced an even greater danger—her own reckless nature and a man who just might be too tempting to resist.

Chapter 5

Storm clouds gathered in the morning sky, their steel bottoms dragging over the mountain peaks, the cold wind heavy with the threat of rain. With Paloma seated behind him, Dante drove his motorcycle along the two-lane road toward the Roman bridge, an insistent feeling of urgency increasing with every mile.

Something strange was going on, something involving his sister's death. But what? Nothing added up so far. Lucía had claimed that the prince was trying to kill her. The coroner said she'd died of a heroin overdose due to her discolored tongue and lips. But the way she'd bled pointed to a deadly, exotic disease—which didn't make any sense.

Spotting the old stone bridge through the dusky woods, Dante dropped a gear to slow the bike. Everything about her death confused him, and he needed more than a hunch to go on if he hoped to figure it out. But from the nagging dread beating like a war drum on his nerves, he didn't have much time.

Kicking his bike down another gear, he scanned the river's banks. Deserted. Then he shifted his gaze to the bars across the road from the Roman bridge. Their doors were closed, their patio tables and chairs arranged in stacks, thanks to the off-season and early hour. Reassured that they wouldn't have witnesses, he stopped at the café closest to the bridge and parked.

Paloma climbed off the bike, and he exhaled, relieved to put some space between them again. Having her soft, feminine body wrapped around him felt too intimate, creating a distraction he didn't need.

Keeping one eye on the woods bordering the empty bridge, he unhooked the laptop and disks from the rack. "You stay here. I'll deliver this to Miguel."

Paloma pulled off her helmet and shook out her hair. "I'll go with you. I want to meet this guy."

"He might not want to meet you. This isn't exactly legal," he added when she frowned.

"He didn't mind helping us break into the casino."

"No, but you couldn't identify him then."

Her lips pursed. She tilted her head, and the early morning light exposed the dark smudges shadowing her eyes. The sudden urge to protect her stirred inside him, the same push-pull of attraction he'd fought all night. He couldn't deny her beauty. She had looked like a fantasy in the tabloids but was much more appealing in the flesh—softer, more slender and shorter, with her head coming up to his chin. More human. And she smelled good—feminine—making him want to move closer and taste the silk of her creamy skin.

But it was the anxiety in her eyes, that worry line

puckering her brow that wreaked havoc on his defenses, provoking the instinct to do battle on her behalf.

He scowled, alarmed at the direction of his thoughts. She didn't need his protection. She was a member of the royal family, the most powerful people in País Vell. He couldn't start sympathizing with her and forget that fact, no matter how vulnerable she looked.

"I'm hardly going to turn him in when I need his help," she argued.

Dante pulled his mind back to his hacker friend. "He might not believe that."

She canted her head to meet his eyes. "I think *you're* the one who doesn't believe it. Why are you so skeptical of me?"

Where to start? When her father had ordered his guards to fire on his mother? When her brother had murdered his sister? But this wasn't the time for that.

"I trusted you," she pointed out. "I told you about the attempt to blackmail my brother. So why won't you trust me?"

Unwilling to answer that, he adjusted his grip on the laptop and started across the road. "Fine. Come on, then." He'd let Miguel decide whether or not to show.

Still feeling jumpy, he ran his gaze from the woods bordering the river to the town's medieval walls. At the end of the bridge was the high stone *puerta* that had once comprised the entrance to the fortified town. Forbidding watchtowers flanked the opening, their arrow slits and crenellated battlements as sinister as the somber clouds.

"So how do you know this hacker?" Paloma asked from beside him, worry threading her voice.

"I told you. Through Rafe. Supposedly he's some kind of genius—got a degree at MIT."

"So why isn't he working for the government or doing some high-level corporate job?"

Dante stopped at the foot of the arched stone bridge and shrugged. "He's never said." And Dante would never ask. Something had driven Miguel Calderón underground, but it wasn't his place to pry.

The wind gusted again, chasing dried leaves over the path and making the pine boughs creak. Then the shadows shifted beneath the bridge. Dante tensed, his pulse thudding hard as a man emerged on the slope. But it was only Miguel.

The tall, lanky hacker loped up the hill, closing the distance between them with ease. Then his gaze landed on Paloma, and he stopped. He pushed his black-framed glasses farther up the bridge of his nose as he checked her out, a cautious look entering his eyes.

"Are you Miguel? I'm Paloma Vergara," she said, extending her hand.

He shook her hand and mumbled a greeting, then shot Dante a questioning frown.

"We're working together on this," Dante explained, handing him the laptop and bag of disks.

Miguel tucked them under his arm, his gaze traveling to the princess again. "It shouldn't take long. I'll call you when I've taken a look."

Dante gave him a grateful nod. "And you'll cover your tracks? We don't want anyone to know that it's been hacked."

Amusement glinted in the hacker's eyes. "Don't worry. No one will have a clue."

"Thanks. We appreciate that." Dante turned his gaze to the café where he'd parked his bike, that unrelenting feeling of danger prodding him to leave. "We need to go."

Paloma added her thanks to Miguel, and they headed

across the road. "He didn't ask any questions," she said. "Doesn't he care what this is about?"

"Questions can get you killed. In this business, the less you know, the safer you are."

She shot him a startled glance. "That sounds paranoid."

"That's reality. This isn't some fairy-tale kingdom, Princess. At least not for people like us."

She opened her mouth, looking as if she intended to argue. But Miguel called out from the bridge. "Dante, wait!"

"Go ahead," he told her. "I'll meet you at the bike." He turned around and walked back. "Yeah?"

Miguel kept his gaze on Paloma, waiting until she was out of earshot before he spoke. "Just a heads-up. I saw a huge contingent of guards coming into town."

Dante stilled, suddenly alert. "Where are they now?"

"About three kilometers out." Miguel's eyes turned grim. "I haven't seen that many troops in weeks, not since the lockdown after that assassination attempt."

A chill slivered through his gut. And he knew with a bone-deep certainty that those guards were hunting him. "Thanks, man. Be careful."

"Always." Miguel hesitated. "But what's with the princess? You think we can trust her in this?"

"I hope so." Especially now that he'd involved Miguel.

The cold wind gusted again, raising shivers on Dante's neck as he headed across the road. Those guards had to be after him. He'd been caught on camera with the princess, leading them to believe he'd abducted her. Now they would scour the town, searching his business, his house, every bar he'd ever set foot in to smoke him out. And if he were smart, he'd forget that visit to the coroner, hightail it back to his palace and hide.

But with the security noose tightening around him, this might be his only chance to question the coroner about his sister's death.

"What's wrong?" Paloma asked when he reached the bike.

"Nothing yet." But trouble was approaching fast. He pulled on his helmet and climbed aboard. "Let's go see that coroner."

But as he kicked the bike into gear, a heavy sense of foreboding weighted his gut. He hoped to hell he wasn't heading into a trap.

They reached Isaac Morel's residence a short time later. The coroner lived in a three-story building located in the heart of the ancient city, amid a warren of tangled lanes. His office was on the bottom floor.

Dante drove past the residence, scanning the surrounding buildings for signs of a stakeout, then headed up another lane.

"Where are you going?" Paloma asked, leaning closer against his back.

"I want to check out the area first." He cut through a nearby alley and circled around the block, puttering past a man hosing off the sidewalk and a delivery truck at a bar unloading beer. A stray dog trotted past, rooting in the gutters for trash.

Just a typical sleepy morning in País Vell.

So why was this damned premonition of danger warning him to stay away?

Shifting his motorcycle down a gear, he approached the coroner's office again. *Still clear.* Knowing he couldn't keep circling forever, he steered into the alley behind the neighboring building and stopped. They both climbed off, and he pushed the bike behind a Dumpster, angling it for a fast escape. A late-model Fiat occupied the space by the coroner's back door.

Dante removed his helmet, another wave of urgency filling him with doubts. But no one knew their plans. It would take the guards time to reach this street. They could talk to Morel, get the information they needed, and leave long before the guards showed up.

Paloma led the way around the building to the front door. Dante hung back, keeping a wary eye on the street as she rang the bell.

No one answered.

She hit the buzzer again, then shot him a questioning look. "What do you think? Should we try the back? Maybe he can't hear the bell."

"All right." This time, Dante took the lead. He strode back into the alley, went up to the door and knocked. When the coroner still didn't answer, he tried the knob.

It turned.

His heart sped up.

Paloma sent him a startled glance. "That's odd."

"Yeah." His sense of trepidation rising, he pushed open the door and entered a narrow hall. A now familiar stench stopped him cold.

Holding out his arms, he blocked Paloma's path.

"Oh, no," she whispered from behind him. "Not again."

"Yeah." Another dead body. What the hell was going on? "You should wait outside."

"No. I need to see this." Covering her nose with her sleeve, she scooted around him, prompting a reluctant spurt of respect. For a pampered princess, she didn't shirk unpleasant tasks.

His nerves clamoring harder, he trailed her through the unlit hallway to a narrow kitchen and paused to glance inside. Dirty dishes crowded the sink. A wheel of cheese stood on a small wooden table, next to an open bottle of wine. Isaac Morel's last meal?

They continued down the hallway, the wooden floor creaking beneath their feet. Then they entered the coroner's office, a dark, dusty room with file cabinets and cardboard boxes crammed like beehives throughout the space. An old-fashioned pendulum clock hung above the desk, its loud ticks drawing his gaze. It read the correct time—meaning Morel had wound it recently. The coroner couldn't have been dead for long.

The front parlor adjoined the office. Paloma preceded him into the room, then abruptly stopped. Trying not to inhale the stench, Dante checked to make sure the shutters covered the windows and flicked on the overhead light. His gaze shot to the body on the floor.

He swallowed hard.

Like Lucía and César Gomez, the coroner lay in a sea of blood. Steeling himself to walk closer, Dante catalogued the grotesque purplish rash, the way his skin had puffed up like an inflated paper bag. The coroner had chewed off his tongue, leaving his mouth a bloody maw. He'd bled from his nose and eyes.

Paloma made a sound of distress. Her face sheet-white, she bolted from the room.

His own stomach roiling, Dante forced himself to stay put, noting the twisted position of the coroner's body, how he'd stretched out his hand, as if making a final, frantic plea for help. Sickened, he turned off the light, followed Paloma into the office and shut the door. She clung to the desk chair, trembling and gasping for breath.

"What *is* that?" she cried, hysteria making her voice rise.

"Hell if I know." He felt just as spooked. Three people

had died now, all in the same macabre way. "But whatever it is, we need to find out. *Fast*. You search the desk." He motioned to the piles of paper cluttering the top. "See if you can find anything about my sister or that patient you were talking about, the one with a similar rash. I'll look in the files."

He thought at first she couldn't do it. She was shivering so badly, and her face looked so bloodless, he feared she was going to faint. But she sank into the desk chair and reached for the nearest pile, prompting another wave of respect.

He hadn't expected her to have grit. The tabloids had portrayed her as a shallow, irresponsible wild child who cared only about attending her next celebrity-studded event. But apparently there was more to her than that.

Forcing his mind back to the coroner, he ran his gaze around the jam-packed room. Morel didn't use a computer, just an antiquated paper filing system—which accounted for the file cabinets and boxes stacked to the rafters throughout the room.

He headed to the nearest cabinets with a sigh. A few drawers later, he realized that Morel was either incompetent at filing or lazy as hell. Giving up on the cabinets, he tried the boxes nearest the desk, assuming they would contain more recent files.

The pendulum clock continued to tick. A truck rumbled past on the road outside. Dante kept on rifling through the records, but with each succeeding box his frustration grew.

"I found it," Paloma said. "Your sister's file."

Abandoning the box he was searching, he strode to the desk and took the folder she held out. He double-checked for Lucía's name, then removed the papers and folded them up. "Any luck on that hospital guy?" he asked, stuffing the papers into the back pocket of his jeans.

Paloma picked up another sheet of paper from the desk. "I'm not positive, but this name sounds right. Jaime Trevino. The date fits, too. But I can't find the entire report."

Dante reached for the nearest stack of paper. "Have you checked this pile yet?"

"No, I—" A sudden rattle came from the front room. Paloma's startled gaze flew to his.

Dante held his breath and didn't move. For several tense seconds, he stared at the adjoining door, every sense riveted on the front room.

Then the rattle sounded again.

"Damn." Unless the coroner had miraculously come back to life, someone was trying to get in.

His heart pounding, he snapped off the lamp. Then he wove through the cabinets to the window and edged aside the drape—just as several guards darted past in the alley outside.

Paloma leaped to her feet. "Who is it?"

"The police." But why were they here? Why the show of force?

And how were they going to get out? The guards were surrounding the building, making it impossible to escape.

"Upstairs," he said. "We'll use the roof." He flung open the door to the parlor, then rushed past Morel's bloody body to the stairs. With Paloma close behind him, he sprinted up the staircase, taking the wooden steps two at a time.

But his doubts mounted with every step. The guards couldn't have found them this fast. No one had known their plans. Unless Paloma had tipped them off... But why would she? And when had she had the chance?

Pushing back his suspicions, he raced up another flight of stairs. He'd grill her about what happened once they'd escaped those guards.

He paused on the third-floor landing to make sure Paloma was still behind him, then ran up the attic stairs. He shouldered open the door, strode through the musty room to the dormer window and peered out.

No sign of the guards. But they were probably standing too close to the building for him to see.

Paloma joined him at the window, her lungs heaving as she gasped for breath.

"We'll go across the roof to the neighbor's building," he told her. "We can work our way down from there."

"All right."

He checked her low-heeled boots. "Can you climb in those?"

"Yes. They've got crepe soles."

He nodded at that, reassured. "Good. But stay near the apex, where it's easier to walk. And try not to make any noise." He turned the latch on the window and tugged it open. "I'll go first," he added. "Grab my hand and I'll help you out."

He hauled himself over the window frame and scrambled outside. Mindful of the edge of the roof just three narrow feet away, he circled to the back of the dormer and leaned out over the top. A second later, Paloma's head emerged.

"Up here," he whispered, extending his hand. Her eyes huge, her face chalk-white, she reached up and gripped his hand. Clinging to him with a death grip, she crawled out the window and stood. He guided her to the top of the roof.

"You okay?" he whispered.

"As long as I don't look down."

He nodded back, impressed. He'd expected her to balk. "I'll lead the way. Watch your step."

Slowing his pace so she wouldn't stumble, he crept across the red clay tiles. When he reached the adjacent building, he leaped down five feet to its lower roof.

"Still all right?" he asked as he helped her down. Landing softly beside him, she managed a shaky nod, increasing his respect. Despite her obvious fear, she didn't give up.

Still trying to stay silent, he continued across the roof to the neighboring house. Two buildings later, they'd made it on to the roof of a one-story addition, just ten feet off the ground.

Dante peered over the edge at the alley, searching for the best way down. He spotted a stretch of dirt—a flower patch gone to seed. It wasn't ideal, but it beat leaping onto cement.

But then a guard appeared below.

Dante froze, hoping like hell the guard wouldn't look up. The man paced back and forth, peering into the shadows, then finally went around the side of the building and disappeared. But the sound of approaching voices indicated he wasn't alone.

Dante leaned toward Paloma. "Jump right after I do. Then run to the bike. No matter what happens, don't stop. We won't have much time." He held her gaze. "Ready?"

Her full lips tightening, she gave him a nod. His adrenaline surging, he scooted to the edge of the roof and leaped.

He landed in the dirt with a heavy thump, the impact jolting through his legs and clacking his jaw. He jumped up and whipped around, just as Paloma came crashing down. She hit the ground and gasped.

He grabbed her hand and yanked her upright, knowing the guards would have heard them land. Still hauling her with him, he raced toward the Dumpster where he'd parked his bike.

But a man shouted out. Swearing, Dante pulled her behind the Dumpster and ducked. A shot barked out, pinging off the metal just inches from where they stood. His pulse chaotic, Dante hopped on the bike and cranked the throttle as Paloma swung up behind him and clutched his waist.

He rammed the bike into gear and gunned the engine, rocketing down the alley just as a barrage of gunfire broke out. Praying the shots would miss them, he sped to the nearest street and turned. Then he took the bike to the limit, zigzagging through the crooked streets toward his estate.

Several minutes later, when he was sure the guards weren't behind them, he exhaled and forced himself to breath. They'd escaped.

For now.

But even as he distanced them from the royal guards, he couldn't outrun his doubts. No one had seen them at the river. No one had followed them to the coroner's house. And yet the guards had surrounded the building and shot at them, as if they'd divined their plans.

And he could no longer ignore the conclusion staring him point-blank in the face. The princess *must* have betrayed them—but how?

He clenched his teeth, a hot blaze of fury scorching his gut. He knew one thing. As soon as they got to safety, he was going to find out.

By the time they arrived at his estate, Dante was hanging on to his temper by the barest thread. He waited until Paloma entered the courtyard, then pushed his motorcycle inside, letting the door slam shut with a resounding thud. Not trusting himself to speak, he set the kickstand on the bike, stalked to the long bank of windows in the living room and glared out. Thunderclouds gathered in the morning sky, as black and forbidding as his mood.

Paloma joined him at the window an instant later. His jaw like steel, he trained his gaze on her. The guilt in her eyes confirmed his suspicions, telling him everything he needed to know.

"I called my brother," she admitted, hugging her arms. "Just before we left. I told him you hadn't kidnapped me and asked him to call off the guards."

He worked his jaw. "You told him where we were going?"

"I…yes. But this couldn't have been his fault."

She couldn't be serious. "Just how the hell do you figure that?"

Misery filled her eyes. "I don't know. But he couldn't have been responsible for this. Someone must have made a mistake."

Incredulity made his voice rise. "You're defending him? After he nearly had us killed?"

"I realize that's how it looks."

"That's how it *is*."

"No, it's not. That's insane. My brother would *never* try to kill me!"

"I hate to break it to you, Princess, but he just did."

Her jaw turning mulish, she shook her head. "Look, even if you believe he has it in him—and I certainly don't—what would he have to gain? I'm rescuing him from that blackmailer. He *wants* me to find that evidence. He doesn't have a reason to wish me harm."

"So how do you explain the guards?"

"I don't know. Maybe Tristan didn't tell my father in

time. Or maybe the guards acted alone. It's possible," she said when he hissed in disbelief. "Just last month our security chief attempted a coup."

Dante didn't buy it. Not after his sister's death. "You keep telling yourself that and you'll be dead."

Her amber eyes flashed. She braced her hands on her hips. "What is it with you? Why can't you believe me?"

"Because those guards just tried to kill us. What else should I think?"

She slowly shook her head. "It's not just now. You've been this way from the start. It's as if...as if you resent me. Despise me. What did I ever do to you?"

He worked his jaw, struggling to corral the anger, but his tenuous hold on his temper slipped. "You really want to know?"

"I said I did."

"Fine. Ever hear of the Mothers' Massacre?"

Her head reared back. "Of course."

"Well, my mother was one of the women your father killed."

Paloma blinked, her eyes registering shock.

But he leaned even closer, not about to stop. "You remember how it happened, Princess? The king had outlawed demonstrations, but a bunch a mothers decided to defy the ban. They wanted to protest the price of bread. They were desperate. Starving. Hell, I could count my sister's ribs. You lived in a castle, surrounded by luxury, while everyone in Reino Antiguo starved. And your goddamned guards shot them—a bunch of defenseless women. Your father gave the order to fire."

The color leached from her face. "That's not what he said."

"I was there, Princess. I was hiding behind the fountain with my sister, holding her hand. I heard him say it. I saw them shoot." He closed his eyes, the images bombarding him even now. The panic, the screams, the blood. His mother lying lifeless in the plaza, gunshots thundering in his ears. His sister's terrified shrieks. And the overwhelming feeling of helplessness as he fled the scene, trying to save his sister while the guards charged toward them on horseback, their rifles raised to fire.

He clenched his teeth. Shaking himself back to the present, he leveled his gaze at her. "So tell me again, why should I believe *you?* Why should I think the best of you?"

Tears swam in her golden eyes. She reached out, as if to touch his arm, then slowly lowered her hand. "I'm so sorry," she whispered, her voice breaking. "I can't believe... That's not what I heard. I thought the separatists started it, that they were throwing rocks."

"Yeah." That part was right. "That's what they did. They intentionally provoked the guards." The militants had infiltrated the peaceful group, making a cold-blooded calculation to sacrifice the women so they could rally more people to their cause.

Dante despised them all.

"I don't know what to say. My father...he's a hard man. He takes a hard line. He wants to preserve the union at any cost."

"By murdering a group of defenseless women." His voice came out flat.

"I know it sounds cruel. It *is* cruel. And I know we need reforms. The monarchy needs to change. I think it needs to be more symbolic, like it is in Spain." Her eyes pleaded with his. "But it's not up to me. Father won't change the primogeniture laws. So Tristan will inherit the throne."

He turned to stare out the window, resisting the appeal

he heard in her voice. He didn't want to believe she cared. He had too much resentment bottled inside him. He'd spent too many years exacting his own brand of justice and plotting revenge.

Hell, he'd even become El Fantasma, taunting the murderous aristocrats by stealing from beneath their noses and donating their wealth to the poor.

But as much as he hated to admit it, the sympathy in Paloma's voice sounded genuine. He sensed deep down that she cared.

He plunged his hand through his hair and exhaled, the tight ball of bitterness he'd carried for years unraveling a notch. That massacre wasn't her fault. She'd been a child when it happened, the same as him.

"I don't blame you for not trusting me," she continued, her voice still soft. "I still say there was some mistake, that Tristan's message didn't get through. I know my brother. He wouldn't have wanted to see us hurt. But I won't contact him again. I promise. Not until we've figured this out."

Dante gripped the back of his neck. He still didn't want to trust her. She was clearly loyal to her brother. And if she discovered his plan—that he intended to destroy the prince—he didn't doubt she would turn him in.

But at least she could see her father's faults. She wanted to enact reforms. So while her loyalty might be misplaced, it wasn't blind.

"How did you contact him?" he asked.

"I used your mobile."

He pulled his phone from his pocket and removed the battery, then tossed it onto the coffee table beside the couch. He just hoped the prince hadn't triangulated the phone call or activated the GPS.

"So can we start over?" she asked, stepping closer.

She reached out her hand. "I promise I won't contact anyone in my family until we know what's going on."

He stared at her slender hand, his anger ebbing another notch, conflicting emotions knotting his gut. He knew he shouldn't trust her. And he sure as hell shouldn't like her. The blasted attraction simmering between them threatened to destroy everything he'd worked toward for years.

He had to compartmentalize her. Keep this impersonal. He couldn't care.

But as he gripped her hand, the silky feel of her threatening to lay waste to his self-control, he feared it might already be too late.

Chapter 6

Paloma didn't know what disturbed her more—the coroner's grisly death, Dante's contention that her brother had tried to kill them or his shocking revelation about how his mother had died.

Slumped at the kitchen table a few minutes later, she stared, unseeing, at his sister's lab report while Dante prepared them an early lunch. But no matter how hard she tried to concentrate on reading the report, she couldn't stop replaying his words. It was one thing to hear the official account of the Mothers' Massacre, to think of it as an abstract historical event. But knowing two innocent and helpless children had witnessed their mother's death...

The pressure in her chest wrenching tighter, she shifted her gaze to him. He stood at the counter, slicing melons and cheese, his big hands wielding the paring knife with confidence. What had her father been think-

ing? How could he have ordered the guards to shoot?
She understood his antagonism toward the separatists; he
wanted to preserve the unity of the country at any cost.
But to shoot innocent, starving women... He must have
realized what the militants were trying to do!

Unable to come up with an answer, she dragged her
gaze back to the report. But the unsettled feeling churn-
ing through her only grew—because her father had not
only acted cruelly but had also given a biased account
of the events. And if he'd distorted the facts surrounding that massacre, what else might he have deceived her
about? Now she had to question everything she'd once
believed—about her country, her family, herself.

Trying to regain some perspective—and quiet the persistent ache pounding her head—she pressed the heel
of her palm to her eyes. Her father had made a cold-
hearted calculation that had cost some women their lives.
But Tristan would never behave like that. Would he? He
wasn't the rigid idealist their father was.

Doubts swirled inside her, prompting memories
lurking in the recesses of her mind of times when she'd
known that Tristan had lied. Times when she'd suspected
of him acting cruelly—like when she'd found the doll her
mother had given her melted in the fireplace, or when
he'd hacked off her hair while she slept—on the eve of
her first ball. Was she wrong to defend him? Was she
letting her sense of duty—the obligation she felt to protect the crown—blind her to his true nature and lead her
astray?

But so what if he wasn't perfect? He'd done those
things as a child. And that certainly didn't mean that he'd
tried to kill them. She knew him. She'd practically raised
him. He was gregarious, charming, smart—everything

a future monarch should be. And unlike her, he hadn't screwed up his life.

Dante strode back to the table, interrupting her thoughts. He set a plate of fruit, bread and cold cuts on the table between them, brought out silverware and salad plates for them both, then took his seat. "Help yourself."

"Thanks, but I'm not really hungry."

He reached for a chunk of bread, a frown wrinkling his brow. "When was the last time you ate?"

"Yesterday at lunch," she admitted. By rights she should be starving after the night and morning they'd had. "It's just that with everything that's happened..." An image of the coroner's corpse popped into her mind, and she fought down a spurt of bile.

"You'll get sick if you don't eat," Dante insisted. "At least take a few bites."

"I guess." Touched that he cared, she picked up a piece of cheese and nibbled around the edge.

"Have you found anything in the lab report?" he asked, making himself a sandwich.

Still feeling queasy, she turned her attention back to the papers, but the little she'd understood in them had left her even more at sea. "The report's pretty technical. I don't understand it all. But you were right. From what I can tell, Lucía didn't die of a drug overdose. She died from influenza."

"The flu? That's crazy."

"Not necessarily. Influenza can be deadly. The Spanish flu in the 1900s killed over fifty million people worldwide. Some think the death toll was double that."

"Did they bleed and have a rash like that?"

"Probably not." She set down her cheese, feeling ill. Those symptoms still seemed closer to hemorrhagic fever. But the report didn't mention Ebola, as far as she could tell. "I really don't know enough about medical things to say."

Dante swallowed a bite of sandwich and frowned. "I thought you worked at the hospital."

"I volunteer there. But I don't have a medical background. I just visit with patients and read to the children, things like that." Making her as superfluous there as she was to the rest of País Vell. "We need to have a doctor explain the results."

Still frowning, Dante picked up the pages and scanned them as he ate. A few minutes later he tossed them aside. "At least we've established one thing. The coroner lied about how she died."

He was right. "But why?" She sipped her glass of water, trying to figure that out. But like everything else in this mess so far, it didn't make sense. "Maybe he was just incompetent. I can't imagine that he'd want to hide a contagious disease. Look what happened to him."

"But even *I* can't confuse those lab results with a drug overdose. So there isn't any doubt that he lied."

She exhaled, unable to disagree. But what could have been the point?

Dante polished off his sandwich. Then he pushed aside his plate, planted his forearms on the table, and met her eyes. "Okay, let's break this down logically. Three people have died so far. My sister, the casino owner and the coroner, Morel."

"And possibly the hospital patient who died last week, Jaime Trevino."

"Right. So maybe four. And it looks as if my sister got sick first."

"So if this is a contagious disease, you think Gomez caught it from her?"

"It appears that way. Gomez owned the casino, and

that's where my sister worked. So the casino seems to be at the center of this thing."

And with all the people who frequented the casino... A chill shuddered up Paloma's spine. "The coroner could have caught the virus when he conducted your sister's autopsy. Or Jaime Trevino's, assuming he died of the same thing."

"Right." Dante sat back and blew out his breath. "We need to find out how this Trevino guy caught it, whether he went to the casino or not."

"That's assuming he had the virus. Right now we're guessing. I could be wrong about that." She lumbered to her feet with a sigh. Feeling slightly dizzy, she carried the plates to the sink. "We need to notify the health officials. Whatever this thing is, it's serious. They need to quarantine the casino and hospital and contact anyone who might have been exposed."

Dante joined her at the counter and set their glasses down. "There's just one problem. If word gets out that Gomez is dead, we'll never get into his safe-deposit box. They'll freeze his accounts."

And if that surveillance footage was in there, the authorities would confiscate that, too, exposing her brother's misdeed.

Her head throbbing, she leaned back against the sink and tried to think. She had to find that blackmail evidence. She couldn't risk having it revealed. But if she didn't report this horrific disease, more innocent people could die.

She exhaled, not happy with either choice. Her conscience mandated that she report this disease. She had to protect the people no matter what. But if that blackmail evidence came to light, people could also die.

"How about this?" she suggested. "As soon as his shift

starts, I'll call that doctor I know, Dr. Sanz. I'm sure we can trust him to be discreet. I'll tell him about the coroner's death. I won't mention Gomez, just Trevino and your sister. We can fax him a copy of Lucía's lab report and let him decide what to do. In the meantime, we can talk to Jaime Trevino's family and figure out how he died."

And keep looking for that safe-deposit box. But they didn't have much time. Gomez's employees could stumble across his body at any time.

Dante tilted his head. "You can use my fax. I need to call Miguel and see what he found out. But I need to buy a new phone first, in case my line got compromised."

Struggling to ignore the ache clog dancing in her skull, she pushed away from the sink. "All right. Let's go. But let's take Jaime Trevino's address with us. We can stop to see his family after we get the phone."

Dante stepped in front of her and blocked her way. "Not so fast. I'm going alone this time."

"Alone? But—"

"I'll get that phone and come back. You stay here and rest."

Wishing she could do just that, she let out a wistful sigh. "Thanks, but there's no time. Not if there's a deadly disease going around. We can't let anyone else get exposed."

"A couple more hours won't hurt." Shifting even closer, Dante reached out and tucked a strand of hair behind her ear. Her heart stuttered hard, his nearness setting off a flurry of nerves. His dark eyes stayed on hers. "You're dead on your feet, Paloma. You didn't sleep all night and you've got circles under your eyes."

"I'm not—"

"There's a guest room just down the hall. Some of

my sister's things are there. You can shower and put on clean clothes. She was a little bigger than you are, but they should fit. Then take a nap. I'll wake you in a couple of hours."

Lord, but she was tempted. She was so tired, she could hardly stay upright. But standing this close, gazing into his deep black eyes, she was finding it hard to think.

"Besides, it's safer if I go alone," he added. "The guards will be searching for us together."

Her breath hitched, fear stabbing through her at the thought of the royal guards shooting at him. And she realized with a start that she'd begun to care about this man, more than was probably wise.

"I promise I'll come right back," he said.

"You'll be careful?"

His eyes warmed. The corner of his mouth quirked up, firing a streak of heat through her blood. "I'm a thief, Princess. I've been evading the police for years."

"Still…" she whispered, her voice uneven.

His body stilled. His eyes stayed riveted on hers. She inhaled his warmth and heat, the sheer maleness of him barreling through her, holding her in place.

And suddenly his eyes darkened even more, gleaming with a frank sensual awareness she couldn't mistake.

Excitement zapped through her nerves.

He raised his hand again and grazed her jaw. The soft scrape of his knuckle quickened her pulse.

She knew she should move away. The timing was wrong. She had that blackmail evidence to find, those terrible deaths to solve. And no matter how insanely sexy he was, Dante was the last man she should desire. He was a thief, a rebel, the kind of off-limits man she'd been attracted to in her irresponsible days. Another virile bad boy who'd only lead her astray.

But right now she needed to kiss him, more than she needed to breathe.

His dark eyes dropped to her mouth. A lick of arousal shortened her breath. He widened his stance and leaned closer, his big body brushing hers, and anticipation drummed through her nerves.

He stroked his callused thumb down her throat. Stark shivers danced over her skin. Then he slid his hand to the nape of her neck, urging her closer. Breathless, she parted her lips.

Her eyes fluttered closed as his mouth slanted over hers, the too-soft touch like an electrical jolt torching a frenzy of need in her veins. Even more desperate to touch him, she reached up and wrapped her arms around his neck, and pulled him close.

He made a low, rough sound of approval in the back of his throat. His big hands cradled her head, changing the angle of the kiss, drawing her closer against his rock-hard frame. And then he parted her lips with his tongue, the bold, sensual invasion heightening the desire swirling inside her, and a fierce rush of pleasure skipped through her blood.

Her head spun. She wriggled even closer, primal needs pulsing inside her, the need to feel him deleting her thoughts. Their tongues dueled and danced. She stroked her palm up his sandpaper jaw, the erotic texture making her moan.

But he lifted his head and stepped back.

His eyes burned into hers. Her pulse still rioting, she gasped for breath. Why had he stopped? He'd wanted her. She hadn't mistaken the signs. But surprise now flickered through his eyes, edging out the desire.

"I'll be back," he said, his voice rough. "Get some rest." Moving stiffly, he walked away.

She closed her eyes, grabbing the counter for support, feeling completely out of control.

Because suddenly, rest was the last thing on her mind.

Surprisingly, she slept. And as she rode behind Dante on his motorcycle later that afternoon, she had to admit that she felt marginally more human—more rested, cleaner and warmer in her borrowed sweater and jeans. Now, if the aspirin would just kick in and stop that blasted headache battering her skull…

But no amount of painkillers could erase the memory of that kiss. She kept reliving the delirious sensations— the tantalizing feel of his mouth, the erotic scrape of his jaw, the pure excitement she'd felt in his arms. Her entire body ached with a deep, pulsing craving, winding her up like a firecracker ready to go off.

It didn't help that she clung to his strong back, his wide shoulders filling her vision, her inner thighs cradling his hips. She had to battle the urge to lean forward, to wrap her arms tighter around him, and slide her hands down his steely chest….

Dangerous thoughts. Thoughts she definitely didn't need right now. They'd snuck out of the city, barely managing to elude the guards, then crossed into the separatist region of Reino Antiguo on their way to interview Jaime Trevino's family about his death. She had to focus on discovering what killed him—not fantasize about the virile thief who'd kissed her, no matter how intoxicating he was.

Dante banked the bike into a curve. She gazed at the steep forested slopes of the mountains, the verdant valley stretching below them, the ancient low fences dividing the green fields. At least she didn't have to worry about the royal guards catching them here. They stayed clear of the separatist region unless ordered in to repress unrest.

Suddenly feeling uneasy, she glanced at the slate-gray sky. A bone-crushing vulture—Reino Antiguo's ancient symbol—soared beneath the storm clouds, bringing a sudden chill to her heart. She was now in Dante's homeland, enemy territory for her.

It hadn't always been that way. Until the seventeenth century, Reino Antiguo had been an independent kingdom bordering País Vell. But then a dispute over an earlier treaty turned into war. País Vell prevailed, conquering its smaller neighbor, demolishing Reino Antiguo's monarchy and giving rise to the fierce resentment that had lasted through modern times. Not only did the separatists refuse to recognize her family's legitimacy, but they'd formed the outlawed terrorist group La Brigada, a group dedicated to using violence to win their cause. Reino Antiguo's ancient motto, *Morior invictus*—Death Before Defeat—was their battle cry.

The road bottomed out, and they zipped along the valley, passing a flock of sheep, a line of cows lumbering toward a barn, a woman rushing to gather her laundry before the ash-colored clouds dumped their rain. The woman stopped and stared as they rode by, her hostile expression reminding Paloma that strangers weren't welcome here.

Even worse, she was a royal, these people's enemy. Someone the La Brigada terrorists were trying to kill. She just prayed they wouldn't recognize her.

But whether they liked her or not, they were still her people. Reino Antiguo had belonged to País Vell for hundreds of years. And she had a duty to protect them, no matter what they thought of her.

The village came into view, and Dante dropped down

another gear. Paloma turned her attention to the trash-littered streets, the crumbling stone buildings with sagging roofs. They puttered past a bar bearing antigovernment slogans and an outlawed Reino Antiguo flag. Two old men wearing traditional black berets sat on a bench outside, suspicion clear in their eyes.

A dozen houses later, Dante brought the bike to a stop. Paloma dismounted and removed her helmet, hoping they could cut this visit short. Even with Dante's protection, she could feel danger pulsing around her, giving her the strongest urge to leave.

Dante tugged off his helmet, and his gaze collided with hers. Heat ghosted through his eyes, sending another zap of awareness skittering through her veins. Her cheeks warming, she looked away.

Definitely the wrong time, she reminded herself firmly. They had more important things on their minds.

He cleared his throat. "You'd better let me talk. They'll respond to me better."

"You think they'll recognize me?" She couldn't keep the anxiety from her voice.

"Yeah. Your face is pretty famous. But this shouldn't take long. Hopefully we can leave before anyone finds out we're here."

Tension thrumming inside her, she accompanied him down the street. A small dog yapped in a narrow alley. A dirty plastic cup tumbled past, then snagged on a patch of weeds. Paloma caught a glimpse of a young boy staring sullenly from a window, and her heart rolled in sympathy. Had Dante once looked like that?

"Here it is," he said, stopping before an apartment building with graffiti spray painted on the door. According to his records, Jaime Trevino had lived on the bottom floor. Dante rang the bell.

"I'm coming," a woman called in the local dialect, and Paloma held her breath, praying her presence wouldn't scare the woman off.

The woman cracked open the door and peered out. Paloma couldn't begin to guess her age. Forty? Sixty? Her dull eyes, weathered face and scraggly gray hair aged her beyond her years. She wore a shapeless flowered housedress, thick woolen stockings and flat country espadrilles on her wide feet. A toddler wearing a stained T-shirt and a diaper clung to her swollen legs.

"Señora Trevino? I'm Dante Quevedo. I'd like to talk to you, if you don't mind."

Her gaze darted to Paloma, and she froze. "What about?"

"Your husband's death."

Sudden fear flashed in her sunken eyes.

"It'll only take a minute," Dante said quickly. "We just need some information."

The woman shook her head and stepped back. "No. I'm sorry. Go away." The child beside her began to cry.

"Please," Paloma said as the widow started to close the door. "We need your help." They had to find out how her husband had contracted that disease.

She'd already done everything else she could. She'd contacted Dr. Sanz at the hospital. She'd faxed him Lucía's report. And she'd convinced him to examine the coroner's body, send samples to a lab in Hamburg and alert the World Health Organization, in case this was worse than they thought. He would also pressure her father to step up distribution of the annual flu vaccine, on the off chance that it might help.

Now she just had to convince this widow to talk.

"I promise nothing bad will happen," Dante said. "We only need to ask a few questions, and then we'll leave."

The woman hesitated. She studied Dante for a moment, then gave him a nod. *"Entren."* Picking up her daughter, she let them in.

Relieved, Paloma followed her into a small front parlor furnished with a threadbare couch and armchair, a decades-old television set and dozens of religious figurines. But despite the shabbiness of the apartment the worn wooden floor had been polished until it gleamed.

Paloma took a seat next to Dante on the sagging sofa. Jaime Trevino's widow sat across from them in the armchair, her mouth set in a rigid line. The toddler crawled up and hid her face in her mother's lap. An uneasy silence filled the room.

"Thank you, señora," Dante said, still using the separatist's dialect. "We'd like to know what happened to your husband and how he died. He was sick, right?"

She managed a grudging nod.

"What kind of symptoms did he have?" Dante asked.

"He had a headache and fever. He ached all over, especially his back. Then he started vomiting."

Paloma leaned forward. "Did he go to the doctor?"

The woman shrank back, and Dante shot Paloma a warning glance. She had to let him handle this.

The widow fixed her gaze on Dante again. "Yes. The doctor thought he had malaria. He gave him some pills, but it didn't do any good. He just got worse."

"In what way?" Dante asked.

The widow made the sign of the cross. "Something was wrong with him, very wrong. His skin turned yellow with bright red specks. His eyes became red, as if *un diablo,* a demon, was inside. And…he changed."

"Changed how?"

"He got sullen, lethargic. He just sat in his chair, staring out the window, his face like a wooden mask. And he wasn't the same inside." She tapped her head.

"You mean he was delirious?" Paloma couldn't help but ask.

The woman shot her a furtive glance, then directed her words to Dante again. "No. If I asked him a question, he answered. But he didn't know anything—where he was, who we were.... His memory was gone."

For a minute no one spoke.

"Did he ever go to the casino? Was he a gambler?" Dante asked.

The widow sat upright and flushed. "No, never. We don't have money for that. He just went to work and came home. Sometimes he stopped to see his friends at the bar."

Paloma's hopes dove as their theory crashed. If Jaime Trevino hadn't frequented the casino, how had he contracted the disease? A chance encounter with a carrier or something else?

Dante signaled to her, and they rose, thanking the woman for her time. But as they stepped outside the door, Paloma turned to the widow again.

"Señora, we're urging everyone to get a flu vaccine." The widow stiffened, fear once again flashing through her eyes, but Paloma forged on. "You, your children, anyone who had contact with your husband. The free clinics will be giving them out."

When the woman didn't answer, her frustration rose. "Please, señora. We don't want to see anyone else get sick."

Dante stepped in then. "Meet me at the bike," he murmured. "I'll just be a minute."

"All right." Hoping Dante could convince her, Paloma turned and headed down the street. Then she glanced back—just as Dante took out his wallet and handed the woman some cash. The widow hugged him and kissed his hand.

Struck by the scene, Paloma paused. The woman treated him like a hero, not just another *paisano*—the diffidence, the trust, the kiss. Could Dante really be El Fantasma, a revered figure in these parts as the rumors implied? He certainly had a motive—his mother's killing—and the skills.

She mulled that over as she walked along, more certain than ever that she was right. But while it hurt that he wouldn't reveal his identity, she didn't blame him for his distrust. In his place, she would have felt the same.

As she gazed up at the brewing storm clouds, a sudden longing gripped her heart. If only she could lead this country someday. She ached for the chance to reform it, to right the wrongs of the past centuries, and use her family's resources to do some good. But her father refused to change the laws.

And maybe it was just as well. The people wouldn't want her to lead them, even if she could. After her lifetime of screwups, they disliked her too much.

Dante jogged up beside her, then slowed, keeping pace with her shorter strides.

"What did you do?" she asked.

"I asked her to keep our visit quiet."

"You think she'll do it?"

"Probably not, but hopefully I've bought us some time, enough to get back across the border, into País Vell."

She arched a brow. Technically they were in País Vell, but this wasn't the place to argue that. "Any idea what she was hiding?" she asked instead.

"So you picked up on that?"

Paloma reached the bike and stopped. "She wasn't only afraid of me. She acted worried, almost guilty, as if she'd done something wrong."

"Yeah, I got that impression, too, but she didn't say." He picked up his helmet. "By the way, I asked where her husband worked. It was at a pharmaceutical packaging company about an hour from here. Vell Pharmaceuticals."

Paloma's heart skittered hard. Suddenly feeling dizzy, she reached out and clutched the bike.

"Are you all right?" Dante asked, sounding concerned.

Oh, God. She pressed her fingers to her lips. She didn't want to believe it. It *had* to be a coincidence. Because if not…

Should she tell Dante? He already despised her family. This would only make him suspect them more. But he'd lost his beloved sister. They had a deadly disease on their hands. He deserved to know the truth.

Dread gathering inside her, she met his eyes. "No one knows this, but Vell Pharmaceuticals belonged to my mother's family."

Dante turned dead still, his expression suddenly alert. And a chill slithered through her heart.

"Who runs it now?" he asked carefully.

She inhaled, released a shuddering breath. "My brother, Tristan."

Chapter 7

Dante stared at Paloma, an intense rush of adrenaline charging through him at her news. "Your brother owns the pharmacy?"

"It's not a pharmacy. It's a pharmaceutical repackaging firm."

"Meaning?"

Looking reluctant to tell him, she crossed her arms. "They're middlemen. They import bulk medications from the manufacturers, repackage them into smaller containers and ship them to wholesalers around the world. It goes to the pharmacies and hospitals from there."

"That sounds convoluted."

"Maybe, but it's cheaper for the manufacturer that way. And easier for the pharmacies. They don't want to stock huge bottles of pills. A repackager puts the medications into smaller lots they can sell, like bubble packs and vials."

Mulling that over, Dante turned and paced away. But his excitement mounted with every step. This changed everything. It could finally be the breakthrough he needed to incriminate the prince, giving him more to go on than a few vague clues.

Because Dante had no doubt the prince was in this thing up to his eyeballs. And if a worker at his factory had died of that disease, it *had* to mean something big.

Now he just had to find out what.

But he had to be careful. He needed Paloma's cooperation in this. If she guessed his intentions, that he planned to destroy her beloved brother, she would turn him over to the guards or bolt.

He swung around to face her. She stood with her slender shoulders hunched, her troubled gaze on his, and her vulnerability knocked his heart off course. And he realized with a jolt that this wasn't only about revenge anymore. Not completely. Something inside him had changed in the past twenty-four hours. He didn't want to protect only his goal; he wanted to protect *her*. He didn't want to see her hurt.

His stomach sank, decades of resentment for the royal family rising up in outrage at the thought. But like it or not, that kiss had changed something fundamental between them. He didn't see Paloma merely as a princess now, but as a person. A woman. An attractive woman with feelings he was reluctant to hurt. A woman he was beginning to respect.

He didn't want to like her. It wasn't comfortable. It wasn't convenient. And it sure as hell wasn't what he'd planned. But he couldn't deny the truth.

Still, he'd worked too damned hard for too many years

to forfeit his plans for revenge. Her father had murdered his mother. Her brother had murdered Lucía. And no matter what Dante felt for Paloma, he refused to let that killer go free.

Knowing he was walking a tightrope, he headed her way. "You know what this means?" he asked carefully.

A cautious look entered her eyes. "What?"

"The casino isn't at the center of this thing. Your brother is." Her spine went stiff, but he forged on. "Think about it, Paloma. My sister worked at the casino where your brother gambled. Gomez blackmailed him. Your brother sent you there to get the evidence. Now we find out that a worker in his factory died of the same disease."

"We don't know that yet."

"No, but you heard his widow. Trevino never gambled. He couldn't afford to. So if he did have that disease, he got it somewhere else. And the prince is the logical link."

"How could he be? That blackmail evidence has nothing to do with the disease."

Dante couldn't argue that point. *Yet.* Not until Miguel finished decrypting those computer files and located the safe-deposit box.

But he still had to convince her to cooperate. "Look, I know you don't want to think badly of your brother. I get that. But you said it yourself—we have to protect the people before anyone else gets sick. So we have to at least consider that there's a link."

"I still don't see how there could be."

"I don't know, either. And maybe you're right. Maybe he isn't involved. Maybe we'll find out he had nothing to do with this, which would be fine. But we at least need to check it out. You have to admit that makes sense."

"Check it out how?"

"Go visit the company and nose around. See what we can find."

"Try to find evidence against him, you mean?" Her voice was tight.

"Try to find out the truth. Whatever it is. Good or bad." Banking on her sense of fairness, he held her gaze.

She stared straight back, emotions ping-ponging through her amber eyes—denial, doubt, resistance, fear. And then her shoulders slumped like a balloon suddenly devoid of air. She reached up and massaged her eyes.

"All right. We'll take a look. I agree that it looks bad. But there might be another explanation," she said, meeting his eyes. "It could be a setup. He might have an enemy who's trying to ruin him. It might not be what it seems."

He nodded. She'd find out the truth soon enough. He strapped on his helmet and straddled the bike, waiting for her to climb aboard.

But as her hands gripped his waist, warning bells clanged in his mind. Paloma was loyal to her brother. No matter how obvious the connection, she defended him to the hilt. She instinctively tried to protect him—a trait he understood. God knew he'd made enough excuses for his sister over the years.

But when that loyalty collided head-on with the truth, which side was she going to choose?

Could Tristan really have a connection to that disease?

Paloma tramped through the woods behind Vell Pharmaceuticals an hour later, still praying that Dante was wrong. But, of course, he had to be wrong. It didn't make sense. What did he think her brother had done?

The cold wind blew, making the surrounding pine boughs moan and sending icy rain spattering over her head. Shivering, she pulled her borrowed sweatshirt higher around her neck, then hurried to catch up with Dante, who was forging a trail through the woods. She understood his logic, though. Tristan *appeared* to be the link in all these threads—at least for now. And even if that appearance was only an illusion, they had a duty to check it out.

She just hoped that storm held off. She glanced through the swaying branches at the seething gray sky, which was turning more ominous with every step. Bad enough they had to trek through the woods. Worse, she could hardly stay upright, that blasted headache flaying her skull with such a vengeance that she could hardly concentrate. But if those clouds let loose, dumping freezing rain on the mountain slopes, she'd end up sick.

Pulling her sleeves over her hands to warm them, she ducked under a low-hanging bough. Another gust of raindrops whipped her cheeks, and she shuddered at the bone-numbing cold. Then Dante stopped on a knoll ahead. Relieved that they'd finally made it, she joined him and glanced around.

They'd reached a small wooded area on the slope behind the sprawling pharmaceutical complex. The firm's main entrance was on the right. To the left were the repackaging facility and warehouses, flanked by the loading docks. A short series of high-pitched beeps drew her gaze to a delivery truck parked near an open bay. Half a dozen men worked to unload it, using forklifts and dollies to haul the pallets inside.

Dante pulled her behind a bush. He hunkered down beside her, his broad shoulder touching hers. Thunder rumbled close by.

"It's Sunday," he said, his voice low. "The factory

should be closed. It's strange that they're getting a shipment now."

He was right. Except for the men working below them and a handful of cars in the parking lot, the compound appeared deserted—normal for a Sunday afternoon.

Not sure what to make of the off-hours shipment, she blew on her freezing hands. Still shivering, she shifted her weight to minimize the chill seeping through her boots. But the wind blasted again, spitting more rain over their heads, and it was all she could do not to groan.

Several minutes went by. The wind began to pick up speed, adding to her misery. Then suddenly, Dante tensed. "You recognize those guys?"

Gritting her teeth so they wouldn't chatter, she squinted to see the men. Although it was hard to tell at a distance, they seemed to range in age from their late twenties to their sixties, and they all had the Mediterranean coloring typical of País Vell. But none looked familiar to her. "No. Why? Do you?"

Dante nodded toward the men. "See the old guy operating the forklift? That's Gaspar Serrano. And the guy with the red shirt is Paco Roig. They're both members of La Brigada."

La Brigada. The outlawed terrorist group. The group that had tried to assassinate her family last month.

"How do you know that?" she asked.

He slanted her a glance. "I grew up around here. Everyone knows who the members are."

She held his gaze. "And El Fantasma? Does everyone know who he is, too?"

Dante turned dead still. For what felt like an eternity, she didn't breathe. But then his strong jaw worked, and he looked away. "Yeah. Everyone knows. But no one has proof."

Her pulse racing, she inched out her pent-up breath. But she continued to study his profile—his rough-hewn nose, the hard, sloping planes of his cheekbones, the strong angles of his whiskered jaw. Stealing was wrong. If Dante was in fact the infamous thief, she couldn't condone his activities, no matter what the cause. But she had to admit that the thought intrigued her. *Dante* intrigued her. She longed to know more about this sexy, complex man. But this was hardly the time.

And he hadn't exactly confessed.

Still, as she returned her gaze to the compound, a new worry crawled through her mind. Most people in Reino Antiguo hated the aristocracy. But El Fantasma had gone a step further, actively mounting a vendetta against the nobility to cause them harm. And if Dante really was El Fantasma... Could she trust him? Would he keep quiet about her brother's actions at the casino? Or was she being seriously naive?

And what about that kiss? What had that meant? Had he merely suffered a moment of insanity and succumbed to the chemistry sparking between them—or something more?

"Looks like they're done," he said.

The men unloaded the final pallet and closed the hydraulic lift gate on the truck. And another question churned through her mind. "If those men are terrorists, why would they work for my brother? They'd hardly want to help the crown." And why would Tristan hire them? Unless he really was involved in something shady...

A sliver of doubt pierced her heart.

But Dante shrugged. "You said most people don't know who owns this place. And there aren't many jobs around here."

That was true. Jobs in the mountains were scarce. Men either farmed, mined or worked in the shale-oil fields, where production had recently stepped up.

The forklifts disappeared into the warehouse. The men put their dollies away. A second later, they came back out and closed the sliding bay doors. Then one man jumped into the delivery truck and drove it around to the parking lot while the others walked back to their cars. Within minutes, their engines started up, and they drove away.

"What now?" she asked as the sound of their motors faded, replaced by the rustle of leaves.

Dante rose, then extended his hand and pulled her up. "I want to see inside."

"Isn't there security. A guard, maybe?"

"Probably." He nodded toward the parking lot, where only one car remained. "But it won't take long to deal with him. I'll let the surveillance camera pick me up. Then, when he comes to investigate…" He shrugged.

Not happy with that idea, Paloma frowned. "What if he triggers an alarm first?"

"He probably will. But it's an hour to the nearest village, and farther than that to País Vell."

"So?"

"So we'll have time to nose around and get out before anyone else shows up."

Uneasy, she shook her head. "I don't know." Why risk another arrest?

"Look, if you're worried about getting caught on camera, you can wait for me here. I'll go in alone."

She vacillated, tempted to let him, but she couldn't take the easy way out. "No. If this has anything to do with my brother, I need to know." Besides, she'd already appeared at the scene of two dead bodies. What did breaking into her brother's company matter now?

But as she set off with him down the slope, more doubts crowded her mind. Dante struck her as a careful man. If she was right about him, he'd spent nearly two decades working as El Fantasma without divulging his identity or getting caught. And if he was willing to break into this pharmaceutical plant without even bothering to cover his tracks, he must suspect they'd find something big.

But what?

A short time later, they stood inside the cargo bay doors. While Dante set the timer on his watch, Paloma flicked her gaze around the cavernous warehouse, knowing the surveillance cameras were recording their moves.

"Let's find the office," he said, striding off.

Her trepidation rising, she hurried to catch up. Bad enough that Dante had lured the security guard into the cargo bay and handcuffed him to a metal post. But somewhere out there, more guards had spotted them on camera. And they would be mobilizing their forces right now, charging toward the complex to arrest them....

She battled down a flurry of dread.

Thunder rumbled outside. Growing even more anxious, she jogged down the warehouse aisle beside Dante, her footsteps cleaving the gloom. The impending storm had darkened the windows, cloaking the room in an early dusk. Crates and pallets loomed on every side.

Dante headed down another aisle, then took a sudden detour, veering toward a metal door. "What's in there?" he asked, peering through the small, high window set in the door. "It looks like a bunch of refrigerators."

"Cold storage, probably. For anything that has to be

kept at a certain temperature, like vaccines. I've seen it at the hospital. The containers have continuous tracking thermometers and a temperature log."

He turned away with a grunt. Paloma pivoted and took the lead, hurrying past miles of shelves and crates. When she finally reached the hall at the front of the warehouse, she paused.

To the left was the entrance to the packaging plant, where the workers bottled and packaged pills. The shipping office was on the right. "This way," Dante said, striding off, and she followed him to the office door.

Dante hauled out his picks and made short work of the lock.

"What are we looking for?" she asked as they stepped inside.

"Purchasing, billing records. Anything that looks out of place." He flicked on the overhead light, then went to the computer at the desk and sat. "Good. It's on. That'll save us some time. Now I just need to find the password...." He started opening drawers.

Still feeling jumpy, Paloma took stock of the office—a drab, dusty room with a stained beige carpet, a trio of wilted plants on top of the metal file cabinets, and vinyl chairs. She peeked out the other door at the reception area—and spotted the surveillance camera aimed straight at her. Startled, she whirled around.

"Found it," Dante said. He pulled a small notebook from a shelf hidden beneath the desk.

"They write their passwords in *that?*"

He flipped through the little book. "People tend to be lazy when it comes to security. You'd be surprised."

Not anymore. Making a mental note to improve her own lax habits, she joined him at the desk.

He typed on the keyboard, and a screen popped up.

"Perfect. They use the same accounting software that I do." He dragged the mouse and selected an application from the screen. Another password later, he grinned. "We're in."

Wishing she could share his enthusiasm, she shot an uneasy glance toward the entrance. She couldn't stifle her mounting dread—that the guards would arrive and arrest them, that her brother really was doing something wrong, that something even more ominous was about to occur.

Thunder boomed, rattling the windowpanes, and straining her nerves even more. "I wish Miguel would call," she said. "This would be so much simpler if we could get into Gomez's files."

"He'll call. Don't worry." His gaze still on the monitor, he slowly smiled. "Here we go."

She dragged her attention back to the monitor, where a spreadsheet appeared on the screen. "What is that?"

"A summary record of orders for the past quarter."

Leaning closer to Dante, she studied the headings on the columns—purchase dates, costs, the names of the medications and the companies they'd bought them from. The wholesaler they'd shipped them to and the marked-up price.

Dante scrolled quickly down the page, making her aching head whirl. She blinked to clear her eyes.

"So what do you think?"

"It looks clean, as far as I can see," he replied.

Thank goodness. She'd hoped this would be a waste of time.

Dante minimized the spreadsheet, then brought up another folder on the screen. A minute later he minimized that one, too. A deep roll of thunder vibrated the floor. Then the skies broke loose, and rain came bucketing down, drumming on the metal roof. She shivered in her damp clothes.

"Shouldn't we get going?" she asked.

Dante didn't look up. "A few more minutes." He continued studying the screen, his expression intent.

She rubbed her arms, amazed at his steely nerves. How could he stay so calm? Tension coiling tighter inside her, she shot another glance toward the door. She couldn't afford to get arrested, especially not here. Not only would the scandal rock the country, but it might reveal the true ownership of the company, a complication her family didn't need.

"What the hell?"

She jerked her gaze back to the screen. "What?"

His brow furrowed, Dante flipped between two screens.

"What is it?" she asked again.

"I'm not sure yet." He brought the first folder back on to the screen. "See this? Everything looks normal. Take this order, for example. Number nineteen fifty-four. Received the first of the month. A shipment of sildenafil citrate—that's the generic name for a popular virility drug—coming from Salvo Pharmaceuticals in Spain."

"So?"

"Now look at this." He switched to the other folder. "The same date. The same quantity of sildenafil, but this one came from Mumbai. Hell, all the shipments in this folder came from there."

"Maybe that's where they manufacture the pills. It's probably cheaper to outsource to India. Then they ship them here for repackaging. There's nothing wrong with that."

He shook his head. "It's the same shipment. They've entered it twice—once as coming from Mumbai and again as originating in Spain. Look." He displayed the two screens side by side. "Everything's the same—the order number, the date. They both contain sildenafil, and the quantity's the same."

An uneasy feeling stirred inside her.

"Why have a separate file just for the goods from India?" he asked. "And look at their profit—what they paid for it versus what they sold it for." He pointed to the original screen. "They made, what? Roughly ten percent profit off the goods from Spain? I don't know much about pharmaceuticals, but let's assume that's a normal margin. Now look at the difference in the Indian goods. The revenue's a thousand percent!"

Her heart sped up. "What are you saying?"

"The Spanish shipments are bogus, a sham. He's importing the medicine from India, but making it look as if it came from Spain. He can hide the profit that way."

"You think he's cooking his books?"

Dante's eyes turned grim. "He's doing more than that. Unless I miss my guess, he's smuggling in counterfeit drugs."

Her jaw dropped. "What?"

"Think about it. The goods are delivered when the plant is closed. You've got La Brigada bringing them in—and everyone knows they run the smuggling routes around here. Then add in the double books..."

Oh, God. He was right. Feeling sick, she closed her eyes.

"It's easy," Dante continued. "And the profit's huge. They make the fakes in India for a minimal cost. They repackage them here, mixing them in with the real goods. That puts them in the legal distribution chain."

And from there, they ended up in pharmacies around the world.

Her belly churned. She felt as if she was going to throw up. Counterfeits were a huge worry at the hospital where she volunteered. They could contain anything— baby powder, sawdust, diluted versions of the real drug. Even if the ingredients were benign, patients could die when they didn't get the treatment they needed for their disease. And if the contents were deadly…

"A lot of terror groups run these rings," Dante added. "It's easier than dealing with illegal drugs. And a hell of a lot more profitable."

"It's despicable." Her voice shook. Was there anything worse than preying on the sick? "I can't believe my brother is involved in this."

Dante's gaze hardened. "Then let's get proof."

His watch beeped. Ignoring it, he swiveled around and jabbed his finger at the screen. "Here's today's shipment, the stuff we just watched them unload. More sildenafil. And it's been entered twice—once as coming from Spain, and again from India."

He hit Print and rose. After turning off the monitor, he grabbed the pages from the printer and strode to the office door. "Come on. Let's go look at that shipment."

She hurried with him through the hallway, denials warring with her growing doubts. She didn't want to believe it. Even the idea of it made her sick. But she couldn't stop the flood of memories—her brother's sly lies, which he'd always covered with a charming grin. The fleeting flashes of cruelty she'd glimpsed—before she'd convinced herself she'd imagined them. But was Tristan truly capable of this?

They sprinted back into the warehouse, then raced down the aisle to the stack of pallets near the cargo bay doors.

"You grab the paperwork," Dante told her. "I'm going to open the pallet and see what's inside."

Her tension mounting, knowing the police could show up at any time, she rushed around the pallet and searched for the plastic pouch. She ripped it off and took out the pages folded inside while Dante grabbed several tools. Then he sliced away the shrink-wrap, exposing the crate.

She glanced at the various papers—the bill of lading, the packing slip and customs forms. She found the name of the shipping company, the weight, quantity and description of the goods. Sildenafil.

Dante pried off the top of the crate, and they peered inside. Dozens of huge plastic containers filled the box. He cut through the packing material on one and unscrewed the lid, then scooped up a handful of pills.

Blue, diamond-shaped pills.

Her heart thudding, she took one from his hand. The word Salvo was stamped on one side; the drug's brand name on the back.

Everything inside her turned cold.

"We'll get them tested," Dante said as a siren rose.

She managed to nod, but she didn't have any doubts. Her brother was a criminal, selling fake drugs.

Chapter 8

Paloma huddled on the rug before the fireplace in Dante's front room hours later, her heart aching, her entire world falling apart. Rain slanted against the glass. Lightning crackled against the sky, flashing like a strobe light in the pitch-black night. She stared dully at the twisting flames, still not able to reconcile what she'd learned about her brother with the man she thought she'd known.

Tristan had betrayed her trust. He was engaged in criminal activities, smuggling counterfeit drugs. They still needed to test the pills, but she didn't have any doubt. Too many details added up.

And it shattered her. It forced her to question everything she believed about him. Her brother, the prince—the future of País Vell's monarchy—was in cahoots with terrorists, preying on innocent people worldwide.

Sick, vulnerable people. The very people who needed hope and help. Could he get more callous than that?

Lightning sizzled again, followed by a deep, thunderous boom that made the worn stone floor vibrate. The power had gone out when the full fury of the storm came down, shortly after they'd left the plant. The storm had provided cover, enabling them to evade the guards and reenter town. But the rain had soaked them on the harrowing drive down the mountain, and not even a hot shower, a roaring fire and the bundle of blankets Dante had wrapped her in could banish the profound chill.

Especially the one in her heart. Because now she had to wonder, if her brother was capable of committing an atrocity like this, what else might he have done?

"Here. This should help warm you," Dante said. Bending down, he handed her a steaming mug of tea.

Grateful, she cradled the mug in her freezing hands, the spicy aroma of the brandy he'd added teasing her nose. She took a sip, savoring the smooth, aromatic heat as it warmed a path down her throat.

"Are you feeling any better?" he asked, lowering himself to the rug. He'd showered, too, then changed into a sweater and jeans. The firelight flickered and danced, emphasizing the clean-shaven angles of his jaw.

"Not really," she admitted. She took another sip of tea, then leaned back against the ottoman beside him and closed her eyes. She felt numb, hollow. Her whole world had tilted off course. "I still don't want to believe he's selling fake drugs."

"It makes sense, though. He probably launders the profits through the casino during his gambling trips. Maybe that's what Gomez was blackmailing him about."

"Maybe. But how could he do something so awful?

He's profiting off people's misery, hurting them when they need help the most."

"I know." Sympathy laced his voice, which she appreciated. At least he wasn't rubbing it in. "I'm surprised he'd need the money, though. Your family owns most of País Vell."

"Most of our wealth is held in trusts—the property, investments, even the businesses, like Vell Pharmaceuticals. We get a stipend from the income, but it isn't as much as you'd think." And Tristan had expensive hobbies and taste. "But there's still no excuse. I don't care how much money he thinks he needs. People can die from those counterfeit drugs."

That news alone would ruin the monarchy when it came out. There would be no way to spin the news into something good. And rightfully not. Tristan didn't deserve a break.

But the monarchy provided stability to País Vell. Its sudden destruction could ignite a civil war.

And she couldn't halt an even greater fear lurking inside her—that he might be involved in something worse.

She pressed the heel of her hand to her gritty eyes, longing to forget about her brother for now. Her head still ached. Her throat was sore—thanks to that icy ride through the rain. And she was so damned exhausted that all she wanted was to curl up before the fire, escape reality and sleep.

But she couldn't ignore the truth, no matter how tired she was. People's lives could be at stake.

And the truth was…she now had to rethink her goal. She'd started off trying to protect her brother, to keep that blackmail evidence from coming to light. And she'd wanted to keep her countrymen from coming to harm—a noble cause.

But Tristan had used her, lied to her. She'd risked her life to get that computer disk. She'd broken into the casino. She'd been chased by guards—guards he'd promised to call off. She could have been shot!

Feeling utterly depleted, she sipped her tea, taking comfort from the warmth. The flames in the fireplace flickered and curled, throwing off welcome heat. The storm raged outside, rain pounding the windows while the lightning flashed.

She slid Dante another glance. He had his head tipped back, his dark eyes closed. Firelight danced on his tawny skin. She allowed her gaze to linger, tracing the potent lines of his face, his frankly sexual mouth, the heavy sinews roping his neck and arms. His stark masculinity washed through her, and her blood began to hum.

He appealed to her, all right. He had an edginess about him, and the kind of raw, animal magnetism she couldn't resist. Her gaze wandered lower, over his hard, broad chest and lean, flat belly to the enticing bulge in his worn jeans. Her face warming, she shifted her gaze away.

And the irony of it all struck her hard. Dante was probably El Fantasma, a wanted criminal, the scourge of the nobility. And yet who was hurting people more? Dante? Or her brother, the prince—a man whose duty it was to lead and protect the people of País Vell?

"What's wrong?" Dante asked, not opening his eyes.

Everything. She swallowed another sip of tea, then sighed. "It's ironic. I've always been the black sheep of the family, the one who couldn't do anything right, while Tristan's been the model son." Everyone loved him. He was everything a prince should be—clever, handsome, refined.

Corrupt.

And while she'd worked for years to help and serve her people, trying in vain to rehabilitate her damaged image, her perfect brother had been committing crimes.

Dante opened his eyes, his expression thoughtful. "How did you end up labeled that way?"

"I don't know." She turned back to the fire with a shrug. "I guess I always had trouble conforming to what my father expected from me. I wasn't very obedient, and he has harsh opinions about a woman's role in life. But things really went south when my brother Felipe died."

"How did that happen?"

She hesitated to say. No one ever discussed that day; the subject was strictly taboo. And she'd spent most of her life trying hard to forget it—not that it had done any good.

But Dante's solid thigh stretched alongside hers. His broad shoulder invited her to lean on him, lending support. She turned her head, and the acceptance in his midnight eyes made her yearn to reveal the truth.

She didn't know why. Maybe she'd held the story in too long. Or maybe with her illusions shattered about Tristan, she already felt exposed. Or maybe it was something in Dante—a man who'd also suffered a life-altering trauma—that made her think he'd understand.

And just maybe it was past time to face down her demons, to dredge up the painful memories and lay them to rest.

She drained her mug of tea and set it aside. Pulling her knees to her chest, she returned her gaze to the flames, and dragged in a steadying breath.

"It happened at the end of the summer. We were hot, cranky and bored that day. My father was busy with visitors, and we were desperate to get out of the house."

"How old were you?"

"Twelve. Felipe was two years older than I was. Tristan was only six."

Thunder rumbled again. The log in the fireplace shifted, throwing up a shower of sparks.

"Our nanny suggested a hike to the lake. My father let us go, but he insisted we take our bodyguard, of course. It turned out they were having an affair, the nanny and the guard. I think...the hike was just an excuse so they could spend some time together. Either way, they were too involved with each other to pay much attention to us."

"You only had one guard?" Dante asked, sounding surprised.

"There wasn't as much danger then. La Brigada hadn't launched an attack in years. And we weren't going far, just to the lake behind the castle. We were still on gated grounds."

She stared into the flames, watching the sparks shimmer and swirl as her mind continued to travel back. "We had a picnic and swam for a while. There was a raptor circling the lake, a hawk. Puffy clouds in the sky." Funny how details like that lingered after all those years.

"The nanny and the guard wandered off. They told me to keep my eye on Tristan, who was skipping stones into the lake, but I got restless. There was a field of wildflowers nearby. I could still see Tristan, so I thought it would be okay if I went over to pick a bouquet."

She swallowed hard. "I got distracted. I sat down and started weaving the flowers into a crown. I could still hear him throwing stones. And then I realized it was too quiet. I didn't hear him anymore. I'm not sure how much time had passed. I jumped up, and he was gone, but I caught a glimpse of him running down the trail. He wanted to find Felipe, who'd gone to climb some rocks."

Her belly churned. Her breath sped up. Sweat moistened her upper lip. "I chased him, yelling for him to wait, but that only made him run faster. By the time I caught up, he'd found Felipe and climbed way out on a boulder. He was standing right at the edge."

Shivering, she closed her eyes. Dante shifted behind her, placing his heavy hand on her shoulder, the solid weight anchoring her somehow.

"Felipe went after him and tried to coax him back. But Tristan didn't understand. He thought it was a game. He dodged him, and Felipe fell. He tumbled off the rock but somehow caught a branch and hung on."

She pressed her hand to her throat, remembering the horror in Felipe's eyes. The absolute panic and helplessness she'd felt.

"I knew I couldn't pull him up. Felipe yelled at me to go for help. I got Tristan off the rock, and then I ran back down the trail, screaming to the nanny and guard. They finally heard me and started running toward me, but they were too far away to help. So I raced back."

"Paloma…"

"No, I want to tell you." Inhaling, feeling as winded as if she'd just run up that trail, she forced herself to go on. "When I got back to the rock, Felipe had managed to pull himself partway up. He was reaching for another branch. I couldn't see exactly. Tristan had climbed back out on the rock and was blocking the way. I could hear Felipe shouting at him to move, to get back. That he was stepping on his hands and loosening the dirt.

"And then…and then…" Shaking, gasping, a cold sweat beading her face, she forced herself to remember it all. "Felipe fell." His high-pitched scream had echoed in her skull—until it abruptly stopped.

For a long moment, neither spoke. Dante slid his hand to the nape of her neck. Then he rubbed her back, the gesture comforting, steadying, helping to dispel the horror she felt.

"Where was the guard?" he finally asked.

She inhaled. "They showed up a few seconds later."

She twisted and met his eyes, feeling as if she were standing on a precipice herself. And suddenly, she wanted to tell him the rest, the horrific truth she'd never revealed. The fear she'd never dared name.

"But just for a minute," she whispered. "When Tristan turned around, there was something in his eyes. I thought…he looked…triumphant. Gleeful. I thought for a second that he'd *made* Felipe fall."

Dante's gaze held hers. For several heartbeats, he didn't speak. Then a log snapped in the fireplace, and she blinked.

"But that can't be right. It happened so fast that I'm sure I imagined that. And everyone said it was my fault. I shouldn't have wandered off. I should have called for help at once."

Dante's jaw hardened, and he sat up. "You were twelve. The guard and nanny were responsible for you. They were the ones to blame."

She exhaled. "I know. My father fired them immediately." Felipe's death had devastated the king. First he'd lost his wife, then Felipe, his heir and favorite son. And he still blamed her. She felt his resentment and condemnation every day.

While she lived with the shame that she'd shirked her duty, that she hadn't saved her beloved brother Felipe.

That she'd survived.

She let out a heavy sigh. "I was never popular, but I became a pariah overnight after that. I tried to make up for it, but I couldn't do anything right. So I focused on helping Tristan instead."

She'd wanted to feel needed, valued. To win her father's approval and assuage the guilt. To prove she wasn't as irresponsible as everyone said. And that maybe she deserved their respect.

"But nothing helped. Everyone still despised me. Any mistakes I made got magnified, until I couldn't stand it anymore. And then…I gave up. I went wild—drinking, drugs. Living down to my bad reputation. Doing anything I could do to forget."

"Did it help?"

"No." She let out a bitter laugh. "I just hated myself more. The tabloids hounded me. My reputation tanked. I was the poster child for dissipated living, giving the separatists a reason to demand independence again. That's what finally made me stop. I didn't care about myself. But I realized the damage I was doing to País Vell."

Dante dropped his hand, but he shifted closer, his broad shoulder supporting her back. She leaned against him, grateful for his compassion. His silence. His understanding.

Somehow it felt right.

"And that's it. That's how I got my reputation." She managed a wobbly smile.

But he didn't smile back. "Paloma, you weren't responsible for any of that. Not Felipe's death. Not Tristan's behavior—either then or now."

Guilt rose like a phoenix inside. "But Tristan—"

"It wasn't your job to watch him."

"It wasn't just that." She inhaled, gathering the courage she needed to voice her deepest fear. "I'd raised him,

Dante. After my mother died, I was practically a mother to him. And if he could do something that atrocious… it had to be my fault. It had to be because of *me*. That I was lacking somehow."

Dante's eyes flashed fire. "You were a kid. You needed a mother yourself. What was your father doing during all that time?"

Drinking. "He fell apart after my mother died. I think she'd kept his drinking under control. And without her influence…" She shrugged.

"That was his weakness, not yours." He raised his hand, using his knuckle to brush her cheek, the tender gesture warming her heart. "You weren't responsible for raising your brother," he repeated.

"Maybe not. But knowing that and feeling that are something different."

Their gazes held. Understanding flickered between them. And she knew he'd felt the same loyalty to his younger sister, the same need to protect her from harm.

The moment stretched. Rain pelted the windows, and lightning cracked outside. Dante's eyes held her steadfast, those dark, shimmering pools sucking her in.

She'd exposed her starkest fear. She'd confessed her shame and pain. And she'd handed this man the power to ruin her family, to bring down the monarchy, to accomplish the separatists' cause.

El Fantasma's cause.

She'd never been so vulnerable in her life.

So why did she feel so safe?

His eyes dropped to her mouth. He slowly traced the curve of her lower lip with his thumb, and her heart skipped in erratic beats.

She knew he'd meant the gesture as comfort, compassion. They were two battered souls connecting for an instant in time. But sensual thrills cascaded over her skin. Her breath backed up in her lungs.

And she desperately wanted to move closer, to inhale his alluring scent, to plunge her hands through his thick black hair. To feel his steel-hard muscles flexing under her palms as he kissed her, his mouth slanting hard over hers.

She wanted to forget the world, forget the pain, forget the treachery of her brother's lies, and simply lose herself in the madness of this man's arms.

His eyes burned into hers. He went stone still, the planes of his face drawn taut. And then he shifted even closer, sliding his hand to the nape of her neck, and she forgot to breathe.

The thunderstorm faded away. The room dimmed, the world receding as her existence narrowed to this one man, this one place, this single moment in time.

His warm breath fanned her face. A maelstrom of need swirled inside her, making it hard to think.

"Paloma," he growled, his deep voice rumbling through her nerves. He reached out with his other hand and cupped her chin, forcing her gaze to his. "You sure you want this?"

She didn't pretend not to understand. This wasn't a game. And it wasn't going to be just one kiss. If they started this thing, they wouldn't stop. There'd be no turning back, no regrets. No blame or lamenting mistakes.

She gazed into his hungry eyes. And she knew right then that she'd never wanted anything so desperately in her life.

"I'm sure," she whispered.

His hard jaw flexed. He splayed his big, callused hand over her neck, sending tremors dancing over her skin.

And then he pulled her against him, prompting a rush of lust in her veins.

Was this an escape? Another rebellion? Was she reverting to her reckless behavior and making a mistake?

Maybe so. But as her eyes fluttered closed and he fused his mouth to hers, she had the feeling that for once in her life she was finally doing something right.

Chapter 9

Dante claimed Paloma's mouth, the lush, moist taste of her provoking an instant surge of insanity and laying siege to his resolve. He knew that he shouldn't do this. She was the princess, his sworn enemy, the woman he was using to get revenge—the *last* person he should have in his arms on this stormy autumn night.

And she was vulnerable right now. Her brother's evil behavior had destroyed her illusions, leaving her emotions raw. He had no right to seduce her during this moment of weakness, no matter how certain she'd said she was.

But none of that seemed to matter. He didn't know why, whether it was her staggering beauty or *her*. But her kiss had plowed through his defenses, obliterating his common sense. It had ignited something primitive inside him, making him want to drive himself so deeply inside her that the world would cease to exist.

He plunged his hands through her silky hair. Then he hauled her even closer, needing to feel her sweetly curving body pressed against his. And she kissed him back, making a wild, sensual sound at the back of her throat that electrified his nerves. He'd never felt such immediate hunger, such a total conflagration of need.

Breaking away from her mouth, he rained kisses down her jaw and neck. She shuddered and clutched his hair. Then her head fell back, her tiny, mewling whimpers sending a rush of heat through his blood.

Struggling to bank the burgeoning hunger, he returned his mouth to hers. Their tongues dueled and danced, the deep, drugging kisses reeling him in. She tasted of brandy and tea and something unique, something so insanely intoxicating he couldn't even stand to stop to breathe.

Tipping backward, he pulled her atop him on to the rug. She let out a low, breathless laugh, then propped herself up on her elbows, and her gaze connected with his.

Time stopped. For several thundering heartbeats he just stared up at her amber eyes, his hoarse breath sawing the air. He took in the perfect lilt of her lips, the mesmerizing line of her throat, the way the golden light carved shadows on her creamy skin. Her luxurious hair framed her face, the satiny mass gleaming in the muted light.

But it was the total trust in her eyes that bulldozed his heart. The honesty. She wanted *him*—Dante Quevedo. Stonemason and thief.

His throat turned thick, a profound feeling of tenderness swirling inside him, a maelstrom of feelings he couldn't name. A need to protect her, defend her, cherish her.

And he knew right then that he was lost. This was far more than casual sex, far more than a momentary diver-

sion, far more than two lonely people seeking comfort in
the night. Whatever the hell was going on here, he was
in way over his head.

Lightning flashed, bathing the room in a silver glow.
Her luminous eyes on his, she sat up, straddling his
waist, and untied the belt of her robe. Then she peeled it
off, baring herself to his gaze.

His heart stuttered hard. His starving gaze devoured
her, worshipping the contours of her breasts, admiring
the play of shadow and light on her tawny skin. She
was full, ripe, *perfect,* her dusky nipples pouting for his
touch.

His breath rasping, he lifted his hands and palmed
her breasts, then ran his hands down the curve of her
waist, over her flat, feminine belly and curving hips. She
arched back and closed her eyes. Her soft moan of need
sent a hot shaft of lust straight to his loins.

His hands unsteady, he gently rolled her beneath him,
then braced himself on his forearms to keep from crushing her with his weight. He continued his exploration
with his mouth and hands until she gasped and whim-
pered with need. Another hot surge of hunger knotted
his guts.

His body pulsed hard, his need growing too insistent
for him to contain. Paloma clutched his arms, her ragged
pants nearly driving him over the edge. The need to be
inside her making him crazy, he inched his way back up.

"You're so damned beautiful," he growled against her
throat. The tabloids hadn't done her justice. Neither had
the nude photos circulating on the internet. She was more
erotic than he'd ever believed, better than any fantasy
he'd ever had. He reclaimed her lips, giving vent to the
violent need inside him, demonstrating how close he was
to the brink.

"Don't stop now," she pleaded when he broke away.

"Just getting rid of my clothes." Rising, he tore off his sweater and flung it aside. He pulled a condom from his jeans, handing it to her as she sat up. Then he made short work of his pants.

She paused. Her eyes skimmed down the length of him, her frank approval exciting him even more.

"Let me," she murmured, ripping open the packet.

He didn't breathe. He couldn't move, every muscle in his body tensing as she took him in her hands.

Then he closed his eyes, the feathery feel of her fingers nearly making him disgrace himself. He gritted his teeth, sweat popping out on his brow with the effort it took to stay in control. She petted and patted and stroked, finally managing to roll the condom on. He was so aroused he could hardly stand.

She took his hand, urging him down. Nudging her legs apart, he settled between her thighs. And then he kissed her again, working his mouth down her body, needing to explore every intimate inch of her, to know her, taste her and brand her as his. She bucked and shivered against him, her soft mewls firing his blood. Still he continued the torture, using his hands and lips and tongue and teeth until she stiffened and gasped.

With a rough growl of approval he spread her legs even farther, then fitted himself to the entrance to her warmth. The slick, hot feel of her as she convulsed around him nearly razed his self-control.

She shuddered and opened her eyes—eyes glazed with the pleasure he'd caused. A fierce sense of satisfaction surged through him, a feeling of pure male triumph and possession—and something more.

His breath backed up in his throat. A sudden feeling of rightness flooded him, as if something in his world had changed. As if a lifetime of barriers had eroded, and this woman, this incredible, courageous princess, was his rightful mate.

As improbable as that seemed.

He lowered his mouth to hers, the kiss unbridled and intimate and wild. Then he slowly, steadily drove inside her, her sleek, wet warmth welcoming him home.

They both groaned.

He couldn't stop. The pleasure was too exquisite, the hunger too insistent, and primitive needs took charge. He began to move, finding the perfect rhythm, coaxing her back to the edge.

He kissed her mouth, her breasts, her throat. She ran her hands down his back, her soft, savage sounds making him crazed. His senses whirled. His breath grew labored and rough. He moved faster, harder, his heart slamming against his rib cage, while she wriggled and thrashed and moaned.

She tensed, then cried out, her inner muscles contracting as she found release. And then he was beyond all patience, beyond all restraint, consumed by a feral madness he couldn't contain.

"Paloma," he breathed.

Her lips parted. Her eyes were feverish, her expression tortured. Urgency overwhelmed him as he lost his final grip on sanity. And then he hurried over the brink, surrendering to the bliss, ecstasy pumping him dry.

But long moments later, as he drifted back to earth, the feel of her sweet body still shivering around him, he gazed at this woman who'd rocked his world.

And he wondered what the hell he'd just done.

Dante awoke several hours later. The fire burned low in the grate. The power was still out, and the candles were languishing in their glass holders, the low flames licking carelessly at their wicks. The worst of the storm had subsided, and lightning flashed in the distance, just a soft rain pattering the roof.

He shifted his weight, careful not to disturb Paloma as he eased out from under her. Then he tucked the blanket around her and slid a pillow under her head.

And for a long moment he just took her in—her plump, erotic mouth; the soft, flushed curves of her cheeks; the perfect symmetry of her finely arched brows. He stroked a stray strand of hair off her cheek, the satiny texture tugging at his heart. She was beautiful. Passionate. Nothing like he'd first imagined.

And completely wrong for him.

He turned away from her with a sigh. Rising, he pulled on his jeans, padded barefoot to the fireplace and moved aside the screen. He added another log, using the poker to stir the embers to life, then leaned back on his haunches and stared into the flames, unable to hold the guilt at bay.

He'd had no damned business touching Paloma. They would never have a future together; the very idea was insane. He didn't have noble blood. He was a commoner, a rebel from the separatist territory. Even worse, he was El Fantasma, an enemy of the crown.

And if all that weren't enough, he was using her to exact revenge. His plan hadn't changed. He still intended to destroy the monarchy, and Paloma was his means to that end.

Except that he couldn't think of her that way anymore. She *wasn't* only the princess, a member of the family he loathed. She was a courageous, spirited woman, a woman her family had badly wronged. A woman who genuinely cared about the country.

A woman he had complicated feelings for.

He scrubbed his face with his hand, his conscience protesting hard. He was using her, all right—just as the rebels had used his mother for their cause.

Which didn't make him any better than them.

He jabbed at the log again and sighed. He'd made a mistake, indulging in the blinding pleasure of her embrace—one he couldn't repeat. Because when she found out the truth...

And she would find out. He couldn't halt the momentum now. She'd already learned about the drug ring. She'd soon discover that Tristan had murdered Lucía just as he'd killed Felipe years ago. And he might have done something worse. Dante had the ominous feeling that whatever the hell the prince was up to, the reality was worse than even he could imagine.

And it would destroy every remaining illusion Paloma had.

Should he tell her? Should he confess everything right now? He tightened his grip on the poker, so damned tempted to do just that—wake her up, reveal the truth and beg her for another chance.

But a chance at what? Exactly what did he want from her?

"What time is it?" she asked from behind him.

He turned his head and looked back. She had propped herself up on one elbow and clutched the blanket to her chest. Her face was flushed, and her long, glorious hair was in sensual disarray, tumbling over her bare shoulders like waves of silk. Her lips were still swollen from their lovemaking; her thickly lashed eyes limpid and huge.

And he realized with a sinking feeling that he couldn't tell her the truth. He couldn't bring himself to shatter her remaining fantasies about her family. Not yet.

"Two in the morning," he said, rising. He set the fireplace poker in the stand and strode back to her side. Then he eased himself down and hauled her into his arms, making sure the blanket stayed around her to keep off the chill.

For a long time, he simply held her, her head resting against his chest, a comfortable silence filling the air. And he realized with a start that he liked being with her like this—inhaling the scent of her skin and listening to her breathe.

And no way was he going to examine why.

After a moment, she sighed. "Listen, Dante. I've been thinking. I know things look bad for Tristan, and that he's probably smuggling fake drugs. But I don't want to tell my father yet."

He stilled. "You want to hide this?"

"No." She lifted her head, then angled around to look into his eyes. "Not at all. We need to stop him. We can't risk having people die from tainted drugs. But right now we don't have enough evidence. Even if we get those pills tested, Tristan could cover his tracks. He's not dumb. He's probably figured out a way to blame it on someone else. And my father won't believe me without proof. I don't have much credibility with him. Tristan has a lot more power and influence with him than I do.

"We have to think about the people, too. When they find out what he's been doing, they're going to revolt. There'll be riots. They could get hurt. And who knows how my father will react to that."

She was right. The king could gun them down, just as he'd done before. But it galled him to protect the prince. He wanted to destroy him, to make him pay for his crimes.

But was it justice if more innocent people died? He bit back a harsh reply.

"I know," Paloma said softly, as if sensing what he was thinking. "It feels wrong not to report this at once. But let's find that blackmail evidence first. Maybe the proof we need is in that. And then we'll decide what to do."

Dante frowned at the fireplace, buffeted by conflicting emotions, feeling as adrift as the shifting flames. He needed to avenge his family. He wanted to protect Paloma. He had to act for the greater good. But how could he do all three?

Not seeing any solution, he sighed. "All right. We'll keep this quiet. But only until we have proof."

Her eyes softened, sparkling with the same gold flecks that shimmered in her chestnut hair. Then she reached up and feathered her fingers over his jaw. "You're a good man," she whispered.

His guilt edged up a notch. "You don't know anything about me."

"You're wrong. I know what this is costing you. My father had your mother killed. I don't blame you for resenting us. I'd feel the same."

Compassion shone in her eyes. And a sudden fullness thickened his chest. She still didn't understand the depths of her brother's depravity. And he needed to tell her the truth right now. He had to own up and confess what he suspected before she discovered that he'd deceived her, and he hurt her even more.

But then she rose to her knees. She let go of the blanket, letting it fall to the floor. She knelt naked before him, her bare skin gleaming in the firelight, her beauty reeling him in.

His lungs ceased to function. He dropped his gaze to her pouting breasts, and her nipples pebbled, demanding his touch. His eyes swept over the sensual curve of her hips, the soft, feminine line of her waist, the sweet paradise beckoning between her thighs.

His throat turned dry, his mind completely blank. Fierce hunger pumped through his loins.

She wasn't what he'd expected. But she was what he needed.

And even if it damned him later, he couldn't resist.

Paloma woke up several hours later, confused. Her throat was on fire. Her eyes felt scratchy and dry, as if sandpaper were stuck under her lids. And that blasted headache lashed her skull without mercy, the pain so piercing she wanted to cry.

With an effort, she cracked open her eyes. She was lying on Dante's leather couch, covered with blankets. The fire had died, leaving the faint scent of wood smoke lingering in the air. Dull gray light seeped through the windows overlooking the valley, indicating that morning had come.

She lifted her hand to her stuffy head. *Great.* She'd caught a cold. Nothing like crashing back to reality after the most fabulous night of her life.

Unless it wasn't just a cold…

That thought startling her, she swung her feet to the floor and stood. A sharp wave of dizziness rolled through her, and she grabbed the back of the couch. Her legs threatened to buckle. Black dots swam in her vision, and as she blinked to clear her eyes, the symptoms the widow had mentioned flashed through her head—the headache, the fever…

No. She couldn't start imagining things. She just needed coffee. Food. Of course she was weak; she hadn't had a decent meal in days. But the thought of eating made her stomach churn, and she fought down the urge to gag.

Still feeling light-headed, she pulled on Dante's bathrobe and cinched it at the waist. She straightened the pillows and folded the blankets, leaving them in a stack on the couch. Then she headed into the kitchen in search of Dante, the stone floor cold on her bare feet. He wasn't there, but the flat-screen television was on, the sound muted. Touched that he'd tried not to wake her, she detoured to the coffee machine and poured herself a cup.

After several deep gulps, she topped off her cup, then stumbled back to the table and sank into a chair. She knew she needed to think about the past night and put it into perspective somehow. Because Dante… She shut her eyes and shivered hard. What a fascinating, virile man.

A parade of erotic images flashed through her mind, and she flushed. That man had *skills*. And she was in way over her head. He was too male, too exciting, too much like everything she'd ever dreamed. Potent. Dangerous. Addictive. A little too wild. *Way* too complicated, given their conflicting roles in life.

And she didn't have time for an affair! She had to find a way to stop her brother and save her people from a potential outbreak of a deadly disease.

The television news came on, drawing her gaze to the screen. Grabbing the remote control, she turned on the sound. Then she continued sipping her coffee, half listening to the headlines, praying the caffeine would ease her headache and stop the dizzy feeling twirling through her skull.

The newscaster didn't mention the coroner's death, which was good. Dr. Sanz must have kept his promise and hushed that up. And there was no news about her supposed abduction, which reassured her as well. Maybe

Tristan had finally come through for her and convinced her father she was fine.

But then what about those guards? Why were they still after her? That part didn't make sense.

The camera switched to a view of the hospital, and Paloma sat up. A reporter stood in front of the entrance, interviewing Dr. Sanz.

"A particularly nasty flu season," the reporter was saying.

"That's right," the doctor said. "We've already seen an upswing in cases, particularly in the south."

"What do you suggest people do?" the reporter asked.

Dr. Sanz straightened his glasses, the gesture reminding her of Miguel. "Basic hygiene is key, of course. Wash your hands several times a day. Cover your face and nose if you cough or sneeze. Stay home if you're sick. Don't go to school or work. And we're urging everyone to get a flu vaccine at once. We're stocking the clinics now. The king has ordered extra vaccines, so there'll be plenty to go around."

Paloma slumped back in her chair, confused. She doubted her father had ordered those vaccines. He would delegate a job like that. So was this Tristan's doing? Was he trying to atone for his mistakes by making sure people didn't get sick? But would someone capable of selling fake pharmaceuticals even care?

Dante entered the kitchen just then, carrying her laundered clothes. Their eyes locked, and he stopped. And his stark male beauty thundered through her, bringing memories of the night roaring back. His mouth ravaging hers. His muscles tensing and rippling beneath her hands. The glorious feel of him moving inside her, driving her to peak after shuddering peak.

"Feeling any better?" he asked, and his growling voice heated her blood.

Her entire body flushed, her mind stalling on exactly how good he'd made her feel. "I'd feel better if you kissed me," she admitted, suddenly breathless.

He didn't move. Heat arched between them, making her heart rate jump.

But then the television switched to a commercial, and the sudden blare of music brought her back to earth. Aware that he hadn't answered, she flushed. "Sorry. Forget I said that."

He shifted his weight, something that looked a lot like guilt moving through his eyes. "Listen, Paloma…"

"No. Let's not talk about it now, all right?" *Oh, God.* He had regrets. And that was the last thing she wanted to hear right now. "Last night was amazing." *The understatement of the year.* "But I don't want to rehash it now."

It stung. She was having a hard enough time dealing with her brother's treachery without suffering Dante's rejection, too. But what had she expected with her bad reputation? A declaration of love?

"We need to talk about it sometime," he said.

"I know. But not now, okay?" Not until she'd had time to erect some defenses. Not until the caffeine kicked in and her head wasn't going to explode.

Hoping to change the subject, she gestured toward the screen. "It looks like Dr. Sanz came through, by the way. They're stepping up the flu vaccines."

"That's good." Still frowning, he set her clothes on the counter, then headed to the coffeepot. She helplessly followed his movements, admiring the flex of his muscled back, the way his worn jeans tightened when he grabbed a mug from the shelf.

She closed her eyes on a sigh. She'd known what she

was doing. They'd succumbed to their mind-boggling chemistry and had sex, nothing more. And no matter how glorious the night had been—or how right she'd felt in his arms—it was done.

"I got a call from Miguel," Dante said, and she looked at him again. "He found the bank account and safe-deposit box. It's in the Banco Pirineo, a small regional bank just over the border in Spain."

Relief flooded through her. "Good. We can head there when it opens and see if the blackmail evidence is inside."

Dante took a long swallow of coffee, then leaned back against the counter and shook his head. "It's not that easy. The bank uses a biometric identification system."

"Meaning what?"

"Meaning they compare your fingerprints to the ones on file. If they don't match, you can't get in."

Her hopes plummeted. "So we can't get at the box."

"Sure we can, but we need to change the fingerprints on file to mine. Miguel's bringing a scanner by. He'll make me a fake identification card, too."

"He can do all that?"

"He says he can. I didn't ask how."

She frowned at that. This certainly was complicated. And what if, after all this effort, the blackmail evidence wasn't there? Trying not to worry, she massaged her pounding temples. "When is he stopping by?"

He glanced at his watch. "He should be here in half an hour."

No time to waste then. "I'll go get dressed."

She rose and grabbed her clothes from the counter. But another wave of dizziness roared through her, making stars erupt behind her eyes.

Dante leaped across the kitchen and grabbed her arm. "Are you all right?"

Nausea roiling through her, she pressed her hand to her mouth. She felt weak, boneless, as if her legs were starting to melt. And that headache! Every strand of hair screamed in pain.

"I'm fine," she lied, trying not to let her voice shake. "I've just caught a cold, probably from that drive down the mountain in the rain. Some aspirin should help."

He didn't believe her. She could see the doubt in his black eyes. And she couldn't blame him. She felt like hell, so miserable she could hardly stand.

But she didn't have time to get sick. She had too much at stake to let a head cold sideline her now.

"I'm fine, Dante. Really," she insisted. "Just point me to the painkillers, and I'll be ready to go."

His eyes still skeptical, he released her arm. She summoned a smile, feigning a strength she didn't feel.

But as she staggered toward the bathroom, trying valiantly to keep herself upright, a sudden vision of Gomez's corpse stole into her mind, and a chill of dread whispered down her spine.

Chapter 10

Paloma was lying through her perfect teeth.

Dante sat beside Miguel at the kitchen table, following her progress with brooding eyes. She puttered around the room, washing dishes and wiping the counters, nibbling at some grapes and cheese.

He knew this woman. He'd memorized her expressions over the past two days and known her intimately last night, so intimately it had taken a long, frigid shower to knock some sense into his head and keep him from doing what his body demanded—making feral, passionate love to her again until they were both too sated to breathe.

He'd miraculously managed to gather some self-control. But even if he couldn't touch her, he still noticed everything about her, including the glaze in her bloodshot eyes, the feverish flush reddening her skin.

Her appetite had disappeared, and the way she wobbled around the room, he feared she was going to fall.

"Your prints are in," Miguel said from beside him.

Dante gave him an absent nod. There was no doubt that Paloma was ill. That drive through the freezing rain hadn't helped, and neither had the lack of sleep. But was there any chance she'd contracted that disease? Could she possibly have come down with it that fast? He'd been just as exposed as she had, and he felt fine.

"You're now César Gomez," Miguel continued, drawing his attention back to him. "Six-two, one hundred eighty pounds." He flipped to another screen, and Dante's photo appeared. "Here you are. As long as no one at the bank remembers him, you're good to go."

"Thanks." Dante's fingerprints were now in the system, replacing the ones Gomez had on file. He'd practiced Gomez's signature, memorized the answers to his personal questions and obtained a fake ID. "Anything else we need to do?"

"No. I just need to cover my tracks so they don't find my trail in their system, and then we're done."

"Great."

Miguel continued tapping the keyboard and flipping through various screens. His thoughts arrowing back to Paloma, Dante rose and joined her at the sink.

Heat poured off her satin skin. A fine sheen of sweat glistened on her upper lip. Circles darkened her blood-shot eyes, evidence of her fatigue.

Despite his vow to resist her, he ran his knuckle along her jaw, her unnatural warmth making his belly clench. "How do you feel?" he asked.

"Better. That aspirin helped."

The hell it did. "You're a terrible liar," he said, and

she flushed. "You need to rest. Stay here and take a nap while I go to the bank. I'll come right back."

"No. I'm coming with you."

Didn't she trust him? He searched her gaze, knowing she had every right to have doubts. She'd shared her body, her heart, her fears, while he still harbored secrets that were going to cause her pain.

But her eyes glimmered with concern. She was afraid for him. His heart warmed at the thought. He couldn't remember the last time anyone had worried about him— not since his mother had died.

Moved, he reached out and cradled her jaw. "Stay here, Paloma. I'll be back before you know it."

"I…" She slid a glance at Miguel. Stiffening, she stepped away. "I'm almost ready. Just give me one more minute, and we can go." She beat a fast retreat from the room.

Confused by her hasty departure, he knit his brows. But it was just as well. Her nearness made her hard to resist.

"You *do* remember who she is, right?" Miguel said, his voice tight.

Dante turned around to face the hacker, the hostility in Miguel's eyes putting him on guard. "I'm hardly about to forget."

"Then what the hell are you screwing her for? You tick her off, and we'll both end up in jail."

His jaw hardening, he crossed his arms. "It isn't like that." *She* wasn't like that. "She's not what you think."

"Right," Miguel scoffed.

"She's different. She's on our side."

Miguel shot him a look of disbelief. "Christ. You've got it bad."

Did he? Was he letting his hormones lead him astray?

Uncertainty penetrated his anger, and he frowned. He understood Miguel's concern. He'd been just as quick to condemn her at first. Hell, he'd spent decades waging his own personal war against the nobility, eager to cause them pain.

But Paloma was different. She wasn't the party animal the tabloids portrayed. She was compassionate, loyal, principled. He couldn't be wrong about that.

Could he?

Miguel snapped his laptop closed, unplugged the biometric scanner and rose. Then he loaded up his equipment and headed for the courtyard, pausing in the doorway to glance back.

"I hope to hell you know what you're doing, man. For all our sakes."

So did he.

Dante pulled his motorcycle to a stop just off the Plaza Mayor in the small Spanish city of Piedra Negra and parked. Thanks to their convoluted route through the mountains—down smuggling trails and shepherds' paths—they'd arrived in the city late in the afternoon. The off-road course had enabled them to evade the guards but had done little to calm his nerves. A feeling of impending disaster plagued him, growing stronger as they neared the bank.

What if someone recognized them? What if, despite Miguel's expertise, they triggered an internal alarm? What if he failed to protect Paloma, and she got hurt— or worse?

And what if she really had caught that disease and he failed to get her help?

Battling back a surge of anxiety, he pulled off his helmet while Paloma did the same. She swung down from the bike, then sank onto a nearby bench, not quite stifling her moan. Fatigue lined her face. Tremors racked her slender frame. And from the way she kept clutching her forehead, he knew the painkillers she'd swallowed hadn't worked.

But she hadn't complained, hadn't taken the easy way out and quit. She'd clung to his back, staying on that bike through sheer dint of will on their torturous trek through the mountains.

Giving in to the need to touch her, he lowered himself to the bench beside her and slid his arm around her back. She leaned against him and closed her eyes, obviously too exhausted to protest. "What's our plan?" she murmured, her eyes still shut.

His chest tight, his protective instincts surging, he turned his attention to the plaza's entrance. People streamed through the high stone archway—young couples, women pulling shopping carts, an occasional tourist carrying a camera and map.

"The bank's inside the plaza," he said. Miguel had located it on Google Maps. "I'll go get that disk while you wait here with the bike."

She pushed herself upright again. "I'll go with you."

"It's too risky. I'll be less noticeable alone."

"Then I'll wait outside the bank and act as your lookout. I can signal if something goes wrong."

The corner of his mouth ticked up, and he shook his head. "Nice thought, Princess, but you're famous. If someone takes a close look at you, we're done."

Not able to argue that, she sighed. "All right. I'll stay here and man the getaway bike." She managed a wobbly smile.

A warm feeling flooded his chest, his admiration for this woman soaring even more.

Miguel was right. He had it bad.

Knowing he had to focus, he scanned the street. Pigeons pecked at a patch of dirt. Dishes clattered in a nearby bar. A mother walked past, holding her young child's hand. It was a typical November afternoon in a quiet, Pyrenees mountain town. And all he had to do was walk into the bank, confiscate that blackmail evidence and get back out.

So why couldn't he shake the persistent dread?

"Listen, Paloma. If anything goes wrong, if there's any sign of trouble, head down the street to the corner and wait for me there. I mean it," he said when she started to argue. "Don't do anything foolish. Just wait for me at the corner, no matter what."

Her eyes troubled, she managed a nod. He squeezed her shoulder and rose.

"Dante." He paused and glanced down. "Be careful," she whispered, her eyes dark with fear.

"Don't worry, Princess. I'll get that disk."

And demolish any illusions about him she had.

Realizing *that* was the source of his dread—the reluctance to reveal that he'd deceived her—he walked up the cobblestone street. He wished he could avoid the confrontation, but there was no point putting it off. The sooner she realized his role in this, the better off she'd be.

Resigned to the inevitable, he turned the corner into the plaza, a wide medieval square with porticoes along each side. Keeping his pace measured and slow, and resisting the urge to shoot furtive glances around him like a guilty man, he headed to the bank. A policeman stood guard outside.

Dante's pulse quickened as he reached the door. He nodded to the guard, swung open the bank's glass door, and went inside. After passing through the metal detector, he strolled into the lobby and glanced around.

He was in.

His heart drumming, he joined the short line at the tellers' cage. Pulling out his cell phone, he pretended to check his calls while he scoped out the bank, locating the entrance to the vault, the surveillance cameras mounted on the walls, the emergency exit sign at the end of the hall.

"Next," a woman called.

Dante approached the teller, a dark-haired woman in her early twenties, wearing too much makeup and a low-cut blouse. "I'd like to get into my safe-deposit box," he said.

"Of course. May I see your identification card, please?"

Dante took out his wallet and slid her the fake ID. Knowing it wouldn't bear close scrutiny, he tried to distract her. "It's quiet today," he said.

It worked. The teller leaned closer, providing him with a better view of her cleavage, and he obliged her by checking it out. "I could use some excitement, that's for sure," she said, a suggestive look in her eyes.

He shot her a wicked smile.

Her color heightening, she parted her painted lips. Then she jerked her gaze back to her computer, tapped for a second on her keyboard and slid him back his card. "Right this way," she said, sounding breathless.

She murmured to another teller, who nodded and glanced at him. Knowing the cameras were recording his movements, Dante kept his hands loose, his shoulders and expression relaxed as he followed her to the vault. But he had the acute sensation that he was being watched.

The teller stopped at a cabinet and opened a drawer, then handed him a card to fill out. He wrote down Gomez's name and the date, signed the card with Gomez's signature and gave her another smile.

Her eyes gleaming, she held up her hand to the scanner, and it beeped her in. He did the same, then risked a casual glance back. Three bank workers huddled together in the lobby, and a frisson of awareness crawled through his nerves. Had he somehow tipped them off?

His apprehension climbing, he followed the teller down the polished hallway, her hips swiveling in her too-tight skirt. She stopped before a wall of safe-deposit boxes and inserted her key in one. As he handed her the key they'd found in Gomez's safe, her fingers trailed over his palm, and he struggled not to flinch.

Clearly taking her time now, she opened the drawer and handed him a long metal box. Trying to hide his impatience, he braved another glance toward the lobby as she escorted him to a booth. A man ran past, his suit coat flapping, a frantic expression on his face. *Damn.* What the hell had gone wrong?

"I'll only be a second," he told the teller as he stepped inside the booth.

"I'll wait down the hall. If there's anything you need, just let me know." She whirled on her stiletto heels, then sauntered toward the lobby with an exaggerated swing of her hips.

Dante jerked the curtain closed, his thoughts spinning as he scanned the booth. No window. No way to escape. He swore.

All hell was about to break loose.

Paloma sat on the bench by the motorbike, her tension mounting as the minutes ticked past and Dante didn't return. But she knew he would be all right. He had nerves of steel, years of experience slipping in and out of houses undetected, and enough fake paperwork to fool the bank. Nothing was going to go wrong.

Then a police car screeched to a stop at the curb. She sat bolt upright as several uniformed policemen piled out and sprinted toward the plaza, their black boots pounding the pavement—and their weapons drawn. Alarmed, she glanced around. What had happened? Where was Dante? This couldn't mean anything good.

Then another squad car roared up to the plaza and stopped, and two more policemen leaped out. One cop raced into the plaza, but the other headed straight for her. A surge of adrenaline brought her to her feet.

"Everyone out," he hollered. "Clear the street!"

The pedestrians around her scurried away. Paloma ducked her head, hoping he wouldn't recognize her.

"Go on," he yelled again. "Hurry up. Everyone out right now!"

Not seeing much choice, she started walking toward the corner, moving as slowly as she dared. But more cops crowded the intersection, stopping traffic and directing people away.

She stole a glance back at the plaza. Still no sign of Dante. And now what should she do? If she didn't stay on the corner as he'd instructed, he wouldn't know where to find her. And what if he needed her help? A policeman blew his whistle, the shrill sound nearly detonating her skull as the crowd jostled her along. At the following intersection, she stopped.

Shivering and sweating, her legs so weak she could hardly stay upright, she propped herself against the side of an old stone building and tried to think. She would *not* abandon Dante. Her family had done him enough harm.

Which meant that she had to go back.

But how?

She lurched toward a deserted alley running between the buildings and glanced around. The cops were too busy directing traffic to notice her, so she snuck into the alley and hurried back toward the street where they'd parked the bike. Her footsteps echoed on the stones. An unnatural silence throbbed in the air.

Then a gunshot barked out.

Paloma jerked up her head, her heart somersaulting into her throat. The shot had come from the plaza—where Dante was.

Her pulse racing triple time, she started to run.

She sprinted to the end of the alley, then peeked around the corner at the motorbike, her lungs gasping for air. *Damn it!* Where was he? She snapped her gaze toward the plaza just as he stumbled into view, dragging a terrified woman in his wake.

Oh, no. He'd taken a hostage! Now what were they going to do?

His expression furious, he drew closer, positioning the frightened woman so she shielded him from the police. The cops charged into the street behind him, their weapons drawn—but held their fire.

Now what? How were they going to get away? Even more police converged on the street.

Dante reached the bike. Knowing the cops would shoot the minute he released the woman, Paloma rushed from the alley and waved her arms. "Help! Help!" she cried.

The police swung their attention to her.

Taking advantage of the distraction, Dante shoved the woman aside and jumped aboard the bike. Paloma hopped on behind him as the hostage darted away. A flurry of gunfire broke out.

Dante cranked back hard on the throttle, causing the bike to leap into motion in a cloud of exhaust. Police whistles blew. More shots rang out, and a searing pain scorched her arm, sending her slumping against Dante's broad back.

She'd been shot!

They swerved down the street, the motorcycle smoking and fishtailing badly, while a burning heat devoured her arm. She gritted her teeth, trying desperately to hold on to Dante and ignore the pain. But the bike vibrated and slid, threatening to upend them, a metallic clatter filling the air.

They swerved around the corner, then roared down the empty street, skidding all over. The police had shot out their tire. There was no way Dante could control the bike. Terror lodged hard in her throat.

Sirens rose. More shots rang out. The bike wobbled and shook, the metal rim clanking against the uneven stones. Trying not to pass out, she struggled to beat back the searing pain, but black spots formed in her eyes.

Dante made a sharp right turn, then raced down another street. She clung to his back, too terrified to think. Then suddenly he swerved again and flew down a ramp into an underground parking garage. He slammed on the brakes, and her head snapped back.

"Get off," he yelled.

While she staggered upright, he sprinted down a row of cars. He lunged over to one and expertly jimmied the lock, setting off an alarm that threatened to split her skull. But he flung open the door and did something to make it stop.

"Get into the back and lie down," he ordered, climbing behind the wheel.

Feeling numb, crazed, wondering how her life had turned insane, she dove into the backseat. She barely managed to latch the door as he took off.

"Stay down," he said, barreling back up the ramp. "No matter what."

Bleeding, and in so much pain it was all she could do to keep from crying out, she flattened herself to the floor and prayed.

One hour, two cars and three mind-numbing close calls later, they picked the lock on the back door of a closed attorney's office on the outskirts of town and went inside.

"What the hell were you doing?" Dante demanded, his voice ringing with anger as he shut the door. "Why didn't you wait at the corner, like I told you?"

She dragged in a breath, her own temper badly frayed. "The police wouldn't let me. They were clearing the street. And I was afraid you wouldn't find me if I moved on."

"Find you? You're lucky to be alive. Do you have any idea how risky that was jumping out like that? You could have been killed!"

"So could you," she countered. "Those cops were going to shoot you the minute you got on the bike." Shaken, knowing how close they'd come to doing just that, she hugged her arms.

But pain scorched through her biceps, and she gasped. Dante's gaze snapped to her arm. His jaw turned slack, and he paled. "You're bleeding. They *shot* you."

"I'm fine," she lied as he rushed toward her. "I'm

sure it's just a graze." Which hurt as horribly as her aching head.

His jaw rigid, his big hands trembling, he gently peeled away her bloody sleeve. His face turned whiter yet. "Damn it! Why didn't you tell me you'd been hurt?"

"I haven't exactly had a chance."

His eyes met hers. And the stark fear in them softened her heart. He might despise her family. He might regret their night of passion. But he was worried about her. *He cared.*

"Please tell me you found the disk," she said, hoping to change the subject. "I'd hate to think I got shot in vain."

"I've got it." His eyes were grim. "But we need to get you to a doctor fast."

"Later. It's really not that bad," she insisted. "Just help me bandage it, and then let's take a look at what we've got. We might not have another chance."

His eyes held hers, his desire to protect her clearly doing battle with his common sense. Then he released his breath. "All right. Here, sit down." He led her to the closest chair. "I'll find something to wrap it in."

He rushed into the bathroom and started banging cabinet doors. Within seconds he emerged with a white box. "I found a first-aid kit."

"Don't worry about cleaning it," she said. "We don't have time. I'll go to the hospital later and get them to patch it up."

"You're damned right you will." His jaw bunched tight. He lowered himself to one knee. Then he took out the roll of gauze and wrapped it around her arm, his strong hands gentle and sure.

"So what happened back there?" she asked, trying to

keep her mind off his tantalizing nearness, along with the throbbing pain. "Did they recognize you at the bank?"

He secured the gauze and set the first-aid kit aside. "Hell if I know. I doubt I triggered an alarm. Miguel's too careful for that."

"But there was nothing about you on the news. There's no reason they'd recognize you."

"Unless your brother tipped the authorities off."

A chill scuttled through her heart. If he was right, then Tristan really was trying to kill them—but why? What was he trying to hide? The counterfeit drug ring or something worse?

Knowing that surveillance footage might hold the answer, she met Dante's eyes. "Let's see what's on that disk."

Dante pulled over another desk chair and sat. He stuck the flash drive he'd taken from the safe-deposit box into the computer's USB port and waited for it to load. A minute later, he clicked on the file.

"It's a video," he said. He selected the program to play it and turned it on.

Her pulse quickened as she stared at the screen. Suddenly a corridor came into view, its polished stone floors gleaming under the lights. In the bottom right corner of the screen was a date stamp, recording the time.

Two weeks ago, 11:16 p.m.

Suddenly two men entered the corridor. Her heart thudding, Paloma leaned forward to see. "It's Tristan," she whispered, indicating the tall, light-haired man in the tuxedo. A darker-skinned man in a business suit walked by his side.

"That must be the Third Crescent terrorist he told you about," Dante said.

"So that part was true." Surprising, given all Tristan's other lies. "Except they definitely aren't partying now."

The two men came to a stop. They glanced furtively around, as if checking to make sure they were alone. The terrorist pulled something out of his suit-coat pocket and handed it to the prince. Appearing even more nervous, Tristan shot another glance behind him before taking the item and slipping it into his coat.

Paloma frowned. "Wait a minute. What was that? Could you tell?"

"No." Dante stopped the video, moved the cursor back and played it again. But she still couldn't see what it was. Money? Casino chips? She shook her head. Tristan had obviously tried to keep it concealed.

Then a young woman wearing a waitress uniform appeared on the screen and walked toward the two men. Dante stiffened beside her, and she spared him a glance.

"My sister, Lucía," he gritted out, staring at the monitor.

A bad feeling mushrooming inside her, Paloma returned her gaze to the screen. Were these the last few minutes of his sister's life?

Lucía walked past the men and smiled. Paloma's stomach flip-flopped. The girl's resemblance to Dante was easy to see. A moment later the men followed her down the corridor and disappeared from view. Several seconds passed. The corridor remained empty.

"Is that it?" Paloma asked, confused. "Because I don't see..."

Suddenly Lucía reappeared on the screen, her back to the camera now. But only Tristan followed her this time.

Without warning, Lucía stopped and turned, as if the prince had spoken to her, tilting her head in curiosity as he caught up. Then all of a sudden her expression changed, her quizzical smile fading, her dark eyes widening with fear. She stepped back and whirled around, but Tristan lunged toward her and grabbed her arm, quickly overpowering the scrawny girl. Paloma covered her mouth, her horror growing as Tristan dragged the waitress twisting and kicking across the hall. Shoving open the door to a side room, he muscled her inside, and they both disappeared.

Paloma gaped at the monitor in shock, a horrible feeling of dread constricting her throat. An entire minute went by. Finally Tristan came back out.

Alone.

He strolled away.

The surveillance footage abruptly stopped.

Paloma shifted her gaze to Dante, unwilling to believe what she'd seen. He still stared at the screen, his strong jaw bunched, his breath ragged and harsh, his big hands balled into fists.

And then she knew. "You think he killed her."

His eyes met hers, the fury in them halting her heart. And another revelation slammed through her, making her gasp.

"You've known it all along."

Chapter 11

Her mind still whirling, the implications of her discovery shaking the foundations of everything she'd believed, Paloma stared at Dante, aghast. Her brother had likely killed his sister. That news was staggering enough. But Dante had suspected it all along.

Of course he had. It suddenly made perfect sense. No wonder he'd wanted to help her find that blackmail evidence. No wonder he'd insisted they stick together to figure this out. He wasn't doing it out of generosity, or even self-preservation. He'd wanted revenge.

"Paloma..."

"No, don't." She held up her hand to stop him, feeling utterly betrayed. He'd used her. He'd lied to her—or at least withheld the truth.

Desperately needing space, she rose and paced across the office to the watercooler, ignoring the dizziness racking her skull. Why hadn't she seen it? Why hadn't she suspected his motives more? How could she have been so blind?

Her head throbbing, she poured herself a cup of water, then sipped it and tried to think. Several days ago, her brother had told her about that blackmail evidence and had asked for her help. She still didn't know why he'd involved her, given the horrific nature of his crimes. But that was the least of her questions right now.

Determined to rescue her brother, she'd contacted Rafael Navarro, a former thief and her old school friend's fiancé. He'd suggested Dante Quevedo, who'd been in jail at the time.

She whirled around. "Why had you been arrested?"

His face devoid of expression, he met her eyes. "I'd been asking too many questions about my sister's death. The guards rounded me up and tossed me in jail."

Where he'd stayed until she'd conveniently gotten him out.

"And the blackmail evidence? Did you know about that from the start?" she asked.

"No, I had no idea about that."

"Did Rafe know?"

He shook his head.

"So it was a coincidence. Quite a bonus for you." And how ironic. She had needed a thief to get her into that penthouse—and had chosen a man who was gunning for her brother. And then she'd played right into his hands.

"How did you know Tristan had killed her?" she asked.

"She phoned me that night."

Shock penetrated her anger, and she blinked. "Your sister called you? When?"

"I'm guessing just after that surveillance footage ended."

Her emotions in total turmoil, she sank into the nearest chair. Dante had deceived her. He'd lied to her all along. She didn't want to sympathize with him. But the agony he must have experienced while watching the final moments of his sister's life gutted her heart. "What happened?"

He didn't answer.

"You might as well tell me," she said. She pushed her hair off her face with a sigh. "There's no point in hiding it now."

His mouth tightened, but he gave her a nod. "She'd just finished her waitressing shift. She always phoned me when she was on her way home, so I was expecting her call. But I could hardly understand her. She kept babbling that she'd seen the prince, that he was trying to kill her, and something about shooting or shots. I couldn't get her to calm down. She was hysterical. She kept pleading for me to help."

Pain roughened his husky voice. Paloma saw the guilt in his tortured eyes and could imagine how helpless he'd felt. "What did you do?"

"I drove to the casino like a bat out of hell. I didn't know who to call, because if the prince was involved…"

"No one would have helped you." He was right.

"By the time I got there she was dead."

"You found her in that room?"

"No. I found her in the parking lot, behind the Dumpsters." His eyes turned bleak. "She'd been left there like a pile of trash."

Stricken, she closed her eyes. No wonder Dante despised her. No wonder he'd looked at her with such hatred at the start. She came from a family of murderers. First her father, now her brother.

What a fool she'd been! She'd trusted her family. She'd

given them her loyalty and defended them, thinking it was her duty to protect the crown. She'd rationalized away her suspicions, ignoring their bad behavior, preferring to live with a patriotic fantasy rather than face the ugly truth.

And she'd repeated her mistakes with Dante. She'd suspected he was El Fantasma, a man who'd dedicated his life to destroying the crown. But she'd told him her secrets. She'd given him the power to bring down the monarchy. She'd even made love to him. No, it was worse than that. She'd *fallen* in love with him.

That thought stopped her cold.

Love? Could she possibly be in love with Dante? That was insane. Less than forty-eight hours ago she hadn't even known this man.

But a lot had happened in the past two days. They'd stumbled across two dead bodies. They'd broken in to the casino, this attorney's office and the pharmaceutical warehouse. They'd leaped off a roof, stolen multiple cars and been shot at by the police. And they'd made love....

She pushed that dangerous thought away.

Time had sped up since she'd met him, the intensity of their experience compressing months of mutual discovery into hours. And while she might not be head over heals in love with him yet, she was clearly halfway there.

But he had lied.

And while she'd buried her head in the sand, deluding herself about reality, he'd played her perfectly in his quest to get revenge.

Her head continued to pound. A huge ache formed in her chest. A cough wrenched her throat, a dry, hacking cough that threatened to tear out her guts.

Swearing, Dante strode to the watercooler, then thrust another cup of water her way.

"Here."

Feeling totally drained now, she took a sip. She was so damn tired. *So numb.*

"Look," Dante said. Standing before her, he braced his hands on his hips. "I admit that I deceived you. I suspected your brother was involved. And yes, when you told me about the blackmail evidence, I seized the chance to find out more.

"But I didn't know you at first. I didn't know what you would do about your brother. I thought you were like they said in the tabloids, and that you'd turn me in if you knew."

He shoved his hand through his hair. "And I needed evidence. No one would believe me without proof. All I had was a call from my sister—an incoherent phone call from a delirious drug addict. Who the hell was going to believe that? Then you came along and told me about the blackmail. What did you expect me to do? What would *you* have done?"

"The same thing." That was the worst part. She didn't blame him. In his place, she would have done exactly the same.

Weary, she slumped back in her chair, too overloaded to think. But even if she'd deluded herself about Dante, even if he'd misled her and trampled her heart, nothing else had changed. She still had to stop her brother. She still had to figure out what was happening with that disease.

"All right," she said, pressing her fingers to her aching temples. "Let's forget that for a minute and try to figure this out. We still don't know exactly what happened in that room. And we don't know the terrorist's connection to this."

"He gave your brother something."

"Right. Something Tristan wanted to hide." Something possibly worthy of blackmail? Her gut stilled. "You think Tristan drugged your sister? You said she had a needle mark in her arm."

"The coroner's report didn't mention drugs, only the flu."

Right again. Feeling lost, she shook her head. "And we don't know *why* he killed her, if he really did."

"Maybe he thought she'd witnessed that exchange."

Her mind flashed back to the surveillance footage. "She wasn't in the hallway then."

"But she saw them together after that."

"Sure. And she obviously recognized Tristan. She told you that much in her call. But how would she have known who that terrorist was?"

"She probably didn't. But they might not have wanted to take a chance."

Paloma released a sigh. Poor Lucía. She had been in the wrong place at the wrong time—and had lost her life.

But this explained why Tristan wanted that blackmail evidence—to cover his tracks. It even explained why he'd tried to kill *her;* he'd feared she might turn him in. But why involve her to begin with? Why hadn't he hunted for the surveillance footage himself?

"Listen, Paloma, about last night…"

Her belly lurched. "I don't want to talk about that."

"We have to."

"Not now." Not on top of everything else. She would come to grips with his rejection—and her own foolish emotions—later, when the rest of this madness was done.

But he didn't budge. "I know I lied. And I admit that I used you to get revenge. But last night… I want you to know I didn't plan that. That had nothing to do with this."

She closed her eyes, unable to bear his apology or regrets. "Just forget it, okay? Can we talk about this later?"

His cell phone rang. "Damn it, Paloma—"

"Dante, please. Just answer the phone."

The phone continued to ring. Frustration brewed in his eyes. Then he jerked it out of his pocket and scowled at the display. "It's Dr. Sanz." He handed her the phone.

Grateful for the interruption, she clicked it on. "Hello?"

"Paloma? It's Dr. Sanz." He sounded breathless. "I'm glad I got hold of you. I got the results from the autopsy on the coroner, Isaac Morel."

Her breath caught. "That was fast. Hold on a minute." She switched the phone to speaker so Dante could listen in, then propped it on the desk. No matter what had happened between them, he deserved to hear this news.

"Go ahead," she told the doctor.

"The lab in Hamburg rushed this through," he said. "They'll have to do more tests, but they tentatively identified the disease. It's caused by a chimera organism, a combination virus, part influenza A. That's how it's spreading, like the flu, through close personal contact—coughing, sneezing, touching."

Paloma glanced at Dante. "So Lucía's autopsy report was right?"

"Partly. But this particular strain is more virulent than most. And it has special properties."

She frowned. "What kind of properties?"

"It causes a cytokine storm."

Dante looked as perplexed as she felt. "What's that?" he asked.

"An overreaction of the body's immune system. It causes a person's immune system to work against him. It's exactly the opposite of most diseases. Usually the weaker people die because their immune systems can't fight the disease. But in this case, the stronger the person's immune system is—the healthier he is—the more deadly the virus becomes. So it doesn't just affect the elderly, like the usual flu. It hits people in their prime, the bulk of the population."

People like her.

"It's just like the Spanish flu of 1918," he added.

Which had killed between fifty and a hundred million people worldwide.

Her belly turned to ice. "Is there a cure?"

"No. It's what we call a super-organism, resistant to any known treatment."

Dante swore.

She closed her eyes, appalled. If there wasn't a cure... But then she mentally replayed his words. "Wait a minute. You said it was a *combination* virus. Part influenza and part what?"

The doctor paused. And suddenly, a horrible premonition consumed her, everything inside her rebelling at the news she suspected she would hear.

"Ebola," he finally said.

Her heart stopped. Her mind went blank with fear.

"It's the Mayinga strain of the Ebola virus," he continued, sounding grim. "That's the hottest, most deadly strain there is."

Her mind spinning, barely able to grasp the implications, she stared at the phone. "But how can that be? Where did it come from?"

"That's what we need to find out."

For several tense heartbeats, no one spoke. Paloma struggled to make sense of the news, but the horror of it had hit her hard. "So we have an outbreak of this Ebola-chimera disease?" she finally whispered.

"It appears so. We've had several more people show up at the hospital today. People are getting scared. They should be. There isn't any good way to stop this thing."

"We have to do something," she said.

"We're stepping up the flu vaccines, getting them out to the clinics and schools. I don't know if it will help, but it won't hurt. Maybe if we can keep the influenza part of this suppressed, we can stop the Ebola part, too. But we need to put a quarantine in place. We have to get the sick people isolated right away so this doesn't spread."

He was right. She didn't even want to think of the ramifications of a major outbreak. It was too horrendous to imagine.

"Is there a treatment for Ebola?" Dante asked.

"No, not really. There's an antiviral drug, an experimental vaccine that's been successful in a few cases, but it works only if it's given immediately after the onset of the disease. I'm having some flown in from Germany and the United States and anywhere else it's been developed. But it's only good for forty-eight hours after contagion."

Which meant they needed to get people in for treatment the second the symptoms hit—without causing mass hysteria.

"How much can we get?" she asked.

"Not much," he admitted. "Not nearly enough. We'll need to triage, do a ring vaccination of the family members of people who have been exposed, and health workers, of course.

"There's also an experimental vaccine for Lassa fever," he went on. "That's another type of hemorrhagic fever. They developed it in Canada and the United States to protect lab workers. I can try to get hold of that, too, but there's no guarantee it will work on this."

She heard the fear in his voice, the dread.

"But either way, I need authorization. This is a major health threat—Biosafety Level Four. We need equipment—pressurized suits, a quarantine facility with airlocked chambers, with showers and decontamination rooms...."

And the only one who could provide it was the king. Only he could order the quarantine. Only he could mobilize the forces to contain the outbreak. Only he could close the casino, the schools, and order the health authorities to take charge.

"I'll make sure this happens."

"I don't have to tell you how urgent this is," Dr. Sanz said, his voice trembling. "I've contacted the World Health Organization, but I don't have authority to act alone."

Neither did she.

She stood. "Do what you can to get those vaccines. I'll call you as soon as I've talked to my father."

She disconnected the phone. Silence hung in the room. Her pulse hammering, her hands shaking, she punched in the number of her father's private line.

No answer.

She tried his office line, with the same results.

Feeling frantic, she tried to think. "I need to talk to him directly. I'll never get through on the phone." And by this time in the afternoon, he was usually drunk.

"How are we going to do that?" Dante asked.

Good question. "I don't know what Tristan's told the guards. But the way they've shot at us so far, I have to assume the worst. So there's no way we can enter the castle and approach the king without them stopping us first."

But there had to be a way.

Clutching her head, she tried to think. "What time is it?"

"Six o'clock."

She tried to remember her father's schedule. "There's a state dinner tonight at the castle. It starts at nine. If we can sneak inside without alerting the guards, I can get us into the dinner to talk to him."

Dante pocketed his phone. "I'll get us inside."

"We have to hurry."

"I know a shortcut through Reino Antiguo. An old smuggling path the separatists use."

"Good." She shook her head at the irony. The separatists' illegal activities might help them save País Vell. "But I want to stop at Jaime Trevino's house on the way."

"Why?"

"His widow was hiding something. I can't help but think it has something to do with this disease. And if it helps us stop it…"

Dante nodded. "All right. Let's go."

She started toward the door, but another wave of dizziness blasted through her, and she stopped.

"You sure you're all right?" Dante asked, sounding far away.

Her arm burned. A horrendous pain flayed her skull. And the fear she'd suppressed all day came crashing back.

She couldn't tell Dante the truth. He'd try to stop her if he knew. And her people needed her to be strong. "I told you, I'm fine."

But as they headed out the door, reality settled in on her like a crushing stone. This wasn't a cold. It wasn't even the flu. She'd caught the Ebola-chimera virus.

And the forty-eight-hour window of hope—her only chance to get that treatment that might enable her to survive—was about to run out.

Chapter 12

By the time they arrived in Jaime Trevino's village two hours later, panic gripped Paloma so badly she wanted to scream. Terrifying images kept pinging around like frenzied fireflies in her mind—Gomez's grotesque rash, the nightmarish pools of blood covering his bathroom floor, Morel's puffed skin and severed tongue. Was that what lay in store for her—a death so horrific that even thinking about it made her feel crazed?

Dante pulled the stolen car up to the curb in front of Trevino's apartment and parked. Forcing herself into action, she pushed open the door and jumped out. She wasn't a martyr. Not even close. The idea of dying from Ebola filled her with such mind-numbing horror, she could hardly breathe. Every instinct she possessed clamored at her to run shrieking to the nearest hospital and beg them to save her life.

But sick or scared or not, she had a duty to the citizens of País Vell. It was up to her to protect them. Only she could talk to her father and save them from falling victim to this hellish disease.

And for once in her useless life, she had to do something right.

Her eyes burning, her legs wobbling badly, she preceded Dante to the apartment door. Night had fallen over the mountains, adding to the chill, and she shivered in the frosty air.

Dante leaned on the doorbell, then turned his scrutiny to her. Hoping the shadows hid the extent of her misery, she struggled to look composed. She couldn't tell Dante she had the disease. He would freak out and insist on rushing her to Dr. Sanz for treatment—and she didn't have time. She had to reach her father and convince him to put that quarantine in place—or more innocent people would die.

Including Dante?

Her lungs closed up, the terrible fear she'd suppressed for hours threatening to erupt. They'd kissed. They'd made love! What if he'd caught the disease from her? She'd never forgive herself if she caused him harm.

But he didn't have the symptoms yet. And as long as he got that antidote forty-eight hours from the onset, he would survive.

Still, she had to be careful. She didn't dare risk infecting Dante—or anyone else. By rights she should be quarantined, not running around the country exposing others to the disease. But until she reached her father and stopped her dangerous brother, she didn't have much choice.

Señora Trevino opened the door right then, and Paloma realized instantly that something was wrong. The widow's eyes looked dull. Blood splattered her arms and dress. Her lips were pinched; her expression blank, as if she'd suffered a traumatic event.

"What happened?" Paloma asked.

The widow's numb eyes landed on her, but she didn't speak.

"Señora Trevino," Dante said, pulling her gaze to him. "It's me again. Dante Quevedo. Please tell us what happened."

The widow blinked, as if shaking herself out of a daze. And then her face crumpled and contorted with anguish, her eyes filling with tears.

"Mi hija," she sobbed. Her daughter. "She has it! The disease. She won't stop bleeding. *Dios mio.* I can't make it stop."

Oh, God. Not the child, too. Paloma closed her eyes and hugged her arms, an awful tightness constricting her throat. "Call an ambulance," she told Dante, who pulled out his phone.

"Señora." Hating to press, but knowing they had no choice with other lives at risk, Paloma made her voice stern. "You have to help us stop this. We need to know what happened to your husband, what you didn't tell us before."

The widow's eyes turned wild, fear edging out her grief. She started to slam the door shut, but Paloma lunged forward and wedged her foot inside.

"You have to tell us," she insisted, even firmer now. "We have to stop this disease before anyone else gets sick. Please, for your daughter's sake. You won't get into trouble, I swear."

"I'll protect you," Dante assured her, closing the phone. "I just called for an ambulance for your daughter. We'll do everything we can to save her. Now you need to tell us the truth."

The widow seemed to shrink. She twisted her hands and bowed her head. And Paloma experienced a pang of regret. Her family had caused this distrust. This woman wouldn't believe the princess, a member of the family who'd oppressed her people for years. But she *did* respect El Fantasma—a man who'd dedicated his life to helping the poor. A man who fought for justice, who tried to make a difference in the world. A man who epitomized everything a *real* nobleman should be.

"Jaime didn't mean to do it," the widow whispered, her eyes pleading with Dante's. "It was an accident."

"We know that," Paloma said, gentling her voice. "Nothing bad will happen to you, I promise. Now please tell us the rest."

The woman met her gaze. Her shoulders slumped even more. "He dropped the crate. He was in a hurry because he'd been late for work, and he…he didn't balance the load on the forklift right. The crate fell off, and the medicines inside it broke. He cleaned it up, but he had to hide the evidence. He knew they'd fire him if they found out."

Paloma frowned. "Just for dropping a crate?"

"He was on probation," the woman confessed. "He'd been late so many times. Our daughter was ill. And he couldn't afford to lose his job. There's no other place to work."

"What was in the crate?" Paloma asked.

The woman paled.

"Please." Paloma kept her voice firm. "The truth, señora. We need to stop this disease."

The woman shrank even more. Then she let out a reedy sigh. "The crate contained the flu vaccine."

Dante rocketed down the mountain like a demon shot from hell, jolting through ruts and potholes, blasting through low-hanging branches and careening around harrowing curves. The prince's diabolical scheme shocked even him. The flu vaccines were spreading the disease. They contained a genetically engineered virus—the deadliest type of Ebola grafted on to a lethal strain of influenza. Either one could kill, but together...

He shuddered. It could destroy the country, the continent, hell, the entire world, eliminating billions of people in weeks.

He glanced at Paloma. She sat beside him in the passenger seat, frantically trying to reach Dr. Sanz on the phone.

"Damn it," she swore. "We've lost the signal. First he had his phone turned off, and now this."

A branch scraped the roof of the car, and Dante jerked his gaze back to the trail. The old smugglers' route was half tractor trail, half cow path, barely wide enough for a vehicle to get through. And with no guardrails, no guarantee that the trail hadn't washed out, he had to stay alert.

"We can call when we reach the castle," he said, his teeth clacking as they bounced through another rut.

"We won't need to then. There'll be reporters at the dinner. If I can get to them before Tristan spots us, I can have them spread the word. It's just...I'd hoped to do this quietly so people wouldn't panic." She grimaced. "I think we're past that point now, though."

"Yeah." Every second counted with the disaster they had on their hands.

The tires drummed on the hard-packed dirt. The headlights swept the narrow trail, illuminating the steep mountain slopes plunging away on every side. Dante swerved around a curve, barely managing to keep the car on the narrow trail. But he didn't dare slow. The castle was still miles away.

"Why would he do this?" Paloma asked, sounding incredulous. "What is he trying to prove?"

Dante knew she was referring to her brother. "You have no idea?"

"I can't even conceive of it. It's barbaric."

He couldn't argue that.

"And I feel so guilty," she continued, her anguish clear in her voice. "I told Dr. Sanz to get the word out about the vaccines. If I hadn't done that…"

"You had no way of knowing. No one did. It's not your fault."

"I guess." Her voice sounded small.

"We'll get the word out tonight. That's all we can do right now."

"I know. It's just…" She coughed into her sleeve, and he shot her a sideways glance.

Fear whispered through him, the same nagging suspicion that had been lurking in his mind all day. "You sure you're all right?"

"Yes. I told you that it's just a cold."

Was it really? Apprehension trickling through him, he returned his gaze to the road. She had a headache, a fever. She was dizzy and would hardly eat. Her skin was flushed, her eyes glazed and increasingly bloodshot. And now that cough…

His stomach fell away. He immediately slammed on the brakes.

"What are you doing?" she cried. "Why are you stopping? We have to get to the castle."

"You have the virus."

"No, I don't. I—"

"The hell you don't. Damn it, Paloma. You heard the doctor. You've only got forty-eight hours to get that antidote." He frantically counted back. They were nearly out of time! "We have to get you to Dr. Sanz."

"We can't. We don't even know where he is right now. Please, Dante. Keep driving. We need to go."

He tightened his grip on the wheel, wild terror filling his cells, making it hard to think. Everything inside him urged him to turn around.

But Paloma was right. They were nearly to the castle. It would take too long to drive back. The fastest course of action was to sneak into that castle and demand help.

Because if anything happened to Paloma...

Ice running through his veins, he released the brake. Then he gunned the accelerator, sending the car careening down the path. He couldn't lose her. No matter what else happened, he had to save her life. Maybe they couldn't be together after this. Maybe once this ordeal was over, she'd never speak to him again. Hell, now that she knew he was El Fantasma, she might even toss him in jail.

But no matter what else happened, he refused to let her die.

Determined not to fail her, he flattened the gas pedal to the floorboard and crashed through a sprawling bush. But then a new worry popped into his mind. "You can't climb with your injured arm," he said. "I'll have to go in alone."

"You can't. You'll never get to my father without me." She paused. "Climb up what?"

"The garderobe chute."

"The medieval toilet? That's your plan?" She stared at him. "But...that's impossible."

"No, it's not. I've done it before."

"When?"

"Nineteen years ago."

The car's tires drummed on the dirt. The beams from the headlights caught the glowing eyes of a fox as it slunk into the shrubs. He maneuvered the car through a series of switchbacks, his fingers biting into the wheel. They were nearly there. Just another mile to go...

"That's when my mother's sapphire brooch went missing," she finally said. "El Fantasma's first heist."

"Yeah."

Paloma fell silent. They finally hit a straight stretch, and Dante floored the accelerator again. The car shuddered as it flew down the trail.

And with every passing minute, his anguish grew. *Damn it!*

Why hadn't she told him how sick she was? Why hadn't she asked for help? He glanced at her shadowed profile, and the truth kicked him straight in the throat. Why *would* she ask for help? What would be the point? For years her family had used her, manipulated her to suit their needs. Even the citizens of País Vell had reviled her, blaming her for things that weren't her fault. So why would she think they'd care?

And while no one had worried about her, she'd spent her entire life protecting them. She'd defended her father, her brother. She'd jeopardized her reputation—even risking arrest—for a noble cause. Now instead of getting the medical help she needed, she would sacrifice herself to save her people, no matter what it took.

"How did you do that?" she asked.

Emotions swirling inside him, he glared at the headlights' beams. Her family might not care about her, but he did. And he refused to fail her now.

"Dante?"

Forcing his mind back to her question, he shot her another glance. He'd never revealed his secrets. He'd never admitted being El Fantasma, not even to his sister. But Paloma had more integrity than anyone he'd ever met. And she deserved to know the truth.

"I went through the garderobe chute, like I said. I was working as an apprentice at the time, part of the renovation crew."

Her frown deepened. "How old were you?"

"Thirteen."

"Weren't you too young to work?"

"I'd dropped out of school after my mother died. I'd wanted to become an architect, but that wasn't going to happen, so I apprenticed as a stonemason instead."

"I'm sorry," Paloma said, sounding subdued.

He shrugged. It had crushed him at the time. "Life happens, and I had a sister to support. So I lied about my age. I'd been an apprentice for about a year when we got that job."

"So you were working on the castle?"

"Yeah, repointing stones on the north side, the area around the garderobe chute. I was the only one who wasn't claustrophobic, so they had me do anything that required crawling up the chute." He glanced at her, barely able to make out her face in the dashboard's light.

"Go on," she said.

"The chute has iron rungs inside, a ladder. That's so the medieval gong farmers could climb up and clean it out when the smell got bad."

"Fun job."

Bitterness stabbed through him. "Typical of the nobles, though, making the peasants clean up their crap."

"Don't expect me to argue that point after tonight."

He acknowledged that with a nod. "Anyhow, no one ever removed the rungs. And as luck would have it, the chute I was repairing came out in the king's chamber."

The road abruptly turned. Then the castle came into view on the slope above them, a stark stone fortress ringed by spotlights, its fortified walls towering over the surrounding land.

Dante turned off the dirt track onto a side trail and jostled over the uneven ground. A moment later he stopped. "This is it," he said, cutting the engine. "We can't drive any closer." He put his hand on the door.

But Paloma touched his sleeve, and he paused. "Why did you steal the brooch?" she asked softly. "What made you become El Fantasma?"

He slumped back in his seat and sighed. "Anger, I guess. It pissed me off that no matter what I did, no matter how hard I worked, I couldn't get ahead. And I thought...I don't know. There was something about seeing the castle. It made me think of knights and honor and justice—and how reality was nothing like that. And I got fed up. I decided to do something, to fight back and try to help the poor."

He looked at her, barely able to make out her eyes in the dark. "It seemed noble at the time. Romantic even. But I was pretty young."

Her mouth wobbled into a smile. "You've got a noble heart, Fantasma."

His chest warmed, her words touching something inside him, something he'd kept buried for a long, long time.

But then she opened her door. "We'd better get moving."

"Right." They had a treacherous climb ahead, a sadistic plan to foil. And Paloma needed that antidote fast.

But as he led the way toward the castle, he knew that she was wrong.

She was the noble one.

* * *

A short time later, they reached the moat. Once twenty feet wide and deep, the massive ditch was now overgrown with trees and brush. And except for the small stream meandering along the bottom, it didn't contain any water, making it easy to access the walls. But even without that barrier, the castle loomed above them, a formidable stone fortress, nearly impossible to breach.

"We'll cross here," Dante murmured, keeping his voice low. "The stream's about three feet deep. We can wade across."

"I can make it."

He didn't doubt it. She had to be the most determined person he knew.

But as he forged a path down the slope, grabbing branches to keep his balance and trying to make sure she didn't slip, the reality of their situation hit home. This was it. Once they entered that castle, they'd go their separate ways. Their time together would be done.

His throat tight, battling an emotion he couldn't name, he skidded on a pile of leaves. But he couldn't deny the truth. He'd get her into that castle. He'd make sure that she received medical help and that her brother was locked behind bars. But then he'd leave. She'd go back to her royal existence, and he'd return to his commoner's way of life.

A hollow feeling inside him, he pushed the thought aside. First things first. He had to get her into this fortress. Then he'd worry about the rest of his life.

With Paloma close behind him, he plunged through the sprawling brush. The dense vegetation helped conceal them, but every rustling branch, every cracking twig exploded like a gunshot in the silent night. He hoped any patrolling guards would attribute the noise to animals and not investigate the moat.

A minute later they reached the stream.

"Hold my hand," he whispered. "It might be slippery."

"I'd better not," she said. "I don't want to get too close and risk contaminating you."

His heart wobbled at her concern. "Forget that." Ignoring her muffled protests, he grabbed her hand. The unnatural warmth of her skin brought another sharp jolt to his heart. But he was *not* going to let this woman die. He'd lost his mother, his baby sister. He refused to fail Paloma, too.

Even more resolved now, he waded into the stream. The frigid water—glacial melt from the surrounding mountains—lashed his feet, and he sucked in his breath. Knowing the icy water would feel worse to Paloma, he pulled her through the stream quickly, making sure she didn't slip on the stones. Then he scrambled with her up the slope to the castle wall.

Panting, she leaned against the base of the wall. "What now?"

Now came the hard part.

"Stand back while I remove the bottom stones."

While she pushed herself away from the wall and stepped aside, Dante reached under the garderobe chute, grabbed a stone and began to tug. He'd wedged the rocks in place after his heist so no one would figure out how he'd committed the crime—or connect it to him.

He worked the first rock loose and set it aside, making sure it didn't roll down the hill and create any additional noise. Then he quickly removed the rest. He ducked inside the chute, felt around for the rope he'd hung, relieved it was still in place.

He stepped back out. "All right, here's what we're

going to do. I'll go first. The rungs are on the left, a couple feet apart. There's a rope you can grab if anything goes wrong. About halfway up there's an alcove where we can rest."

"Okay."

Suddenly besieged by doubts, he paused. "Listen, Paloma. I can go up and bring you help. Your arm—"

"I told you. I have to go with you. They'll arrest you if you go in alone. And I can make it. My arm hurts, but it's not that bad."

The hell it wasn't. Not only had she been shot, but that virus was taking its toll. He was amazed she could still stand upright, let alone make a three-story climb.

But she was right. The guards wouldn't let him near the king. Frustrated, he blew out his breath. "All right, but be careful. Stop when you need to rest."

Bending back down, he crawled into the tomblike chute and found the bottom rung. Then he reached up and began to climb. Paloma followed a moment later, her soft breathing breaking the gloom.

Sweat dripped into his eyes. Cobwebs brushed his face, and he swatted them aside. Unable to see his hands, he worked his way up slowly, testing each iron bar for stability before he applied his weight. Several minutes later, he reached the halfway point.

Grabbing the rope for safety, he stepped onto the shallow stone ledge. But his movements dislodged a pile of debris.

Oh, hell. "Watch out," he called out as dirt and stones showered down. They struck the ground almost two stories below them with muffled thuds.

"I'm all right," Paloma answered, sounding breathless. "I just got dirt in my eyes."

He exhaled at the close call. She was lucky a rock hadn't hit her head. "I'm sorry. I couldn't see the debris."

A second later, the air around him stirred. Reaching down, he gripped her uninjured arm and pulled her onto the ledge. She squeezed in beside him, her breath sawing in his ear.

"We're about halfway there," he told her, trying to make out her profile in the pitch-black gloom. "How are you doing?"

"My arm hurts," she admitted. "But I can make it the rest of the way."

Marveling over her stamina, he shook his head. His sister never would have made it this far. She never would have tried. Lucía had been too soft, too fragile. Too weak.

He frowned at the unkind thought, but it was true. Lucía hadn't had half of Paloma's fortitude. She'd drifted through her brief life, unable—or unwilling—to help herself.

And it wasn't his fault. He'd tried his best to help her, but she hadn't wanted to help herself. She'd preferred to be a waif, a victim, content to let others rescue her.

Whereas Paloma charged into the battle and confronted injustice head-on.

And suddenly, the guilt he'd harbored over his sister's death faded away. He hadn't been able to save Lucía. No one could. But Paloma was a fighter. And he'd damned well make sure she survived.

"Let's get going," he said.

Grabbing hold of an iron rung, he resumed his climb. Paloma instantly followed, her quiet breaths mingling with his. He peered toward the top of the chute, unable to see any light, but he'd expected that. Years ago, someone had installed a plank over the opening to block out drafts. He just hoped they hadn't bolted it in place.

An iron rung wobbled in his hand, and he paused. "Be careful of this one," he called down to Paloma. "It's loose."

"I will."

He climbed carefully past the shaky rung. "We're almost to the top," he added, taking another step up. "You'll have to give me a minute to move the board."

"All ri—" She gasped. A loud scraping sound rent the air, stopping his heart. Then rocks crashed against the sides of the chute, and Paloma let out a strangled cry.

Dante stared into the darkness below him, fierce dread flogging his nerves. "Paloma! Are you all right?"

Silence echoed back. Pure panic ripped through his veins. *She'd fallen.* She'd never survive a fall that far. He scrambled back down the rungs.

But then a soft whimper reached his ears, and he stopped. "Paloma?"

"I...I'm all right. The rung came loose. But I caught hold of the rope...."

He closed his eyes, the thought of her dangling over the deadly void hijacking his breath. "Can you reach the rungs again?"

"I'll try." Her voice trembled.

He reached out blindly and gripped the rope. "Hold on. I'm going to swing you back toward the wall."

Clinging to a rung with one hand, he used the other to take hold of the rope and pull it toward the wall. "Can you reach the rungs now?" he asked.

Several seconds passed. The rope undulated as she groped the wall, and he prayed that she'd hold on.

"I found it," she finally said.

He closed his eyes, shaken to the core. "Climb back down and wait for me there."

"But we're almost to the top."

"For God's sake, Paloma—"

"I can make it. I just…"

Another grinding sound filled the air. More rocks ricocheted through the chute, and his heart lodged tight in his throat. Unable to see what was happening, he could only stand by helplessly, despising the powerlessness he felt. But he couldn't save her from above.

"I made it past the bad part," she announced, her relief palpable.

"Right." He managed to draw in a shaky breath. "Let's get out of here."

Hurrying now, he scaled the last few rungs, then felt for the plank overhead. Balancing on the ladder, he shoved his shoulder against the plank. It didn't budge.

Swearing, he tried again, heaving with all his might. The plank gave slightly, then scraped against the stone bench it was resting on. Dante froze, listening for signs that they'd been heard. Several seconds ticked past. No sounds came from the chamber above. Relieved, Dante shoved the plank away and climbed out, then glanced around the darkened alcove which housed the chute. A tapestry separated it from the main room.

He turned back to the chute and peered down. A second later, Paloma's head came into view. He grabbed her uninjured arm and hauled her out, his pulse still refusing to slow. She stumbled against him, clinging to his shirt to get her balance. Overwhelmed by the need to touch her, he pulled her close.

Ignoring her muffled protests, he tucked her head to his chest and pressed his cheek to her hair. Then he closed his eyes, and for a long time he just held her, feeling her slender body quivering against his. She'd nearly died. His throat thick, emotions crowding inside him, he held her even tighter, unable to let her go.

But then she raised her head and stepped back.

Dirt covered her hair. Her eyes looked huge in the low light. She raised her chin in an obvious attempt to appear unfazed, but her quivering lips betrayed her fear.

Still too overcome to form a coherent thought, he brushed a pebble from her hair. "Paloma," he whispered.

"We'd better hurry," she said.

She was right. She needed medical help, and they had a killer to stop. Pulling himself together, he lowered his arms and peered around the tapestry and into the faintly lit room. Certain they were alone, he tugged the tapestry aside, strode halfway into the chamber, and stopped.

"You'd better lead the way," he told her when she caught up. "We're on your turf now."

"Not exactly," a voice said from the shadows behind them, and he froze.

Foreboding skittering through him, Dante turned— and stared straight down the barrel of Tristan's gun.

Chapter 13

Paloma gaped at her brother, her mind reeling, unable to believe he'd anticipated their moves.

"You didn't think I'd figure it out, did you?" Tristan taunted, his brown eyes glittering as he moved closer, his weapon trained on them. "But then, you've always underestimated me."

"Underestimated?" Her face burned, a hot blast of fury driving out the shock. "*Overestimated,* you mean. I thought you were honest. Human. Not a killer preying on sick, innocent people—the people who depend on you for help."

His mouth twisted into a smirk, the face she'd always thought so handsome with his square cleft chin and noble nose sickening her now. "Amazing how you always believed that crap. But it made you easy to manipulate. You were always charging to my rescue, anxious to protect me, so willing to take the blame for anything I did.

And I've played your devoted brother, loyal despite your screwups. I'm so kindhearted. So generous and forgiving. What a prince!" He laughed.

Thoroughly disgusted, she stared at the brother she thought she'd known. He was a sociopath, a monster without feelings, concerned only about himself.

He motioned with his pistol toward the wall. "Now, get over there, both of you. And no sudden moves."

She slid Dante a glance. He stood with his strong jaw bunched, his big hands balled into fists, anger radiating off him in waves.

And a sudden fear jolted through her. She couldn't let him do anything foolish. Tristan would kill him if he did.

"Now!" Tristan barked. He glared at Dante but pointed the gun at her. "Or Paloma's dead."

Praying Dante would listen, that he'd let her handle this, she shuffled back to the wall. Looking as if the effort cost him, Dante finally did the same.

"That's better." Tristan flicked on a table lamp. The bright light flooded the room, making her blink. "Now, empty your pockets," he said. "Put everything on the floor and kick it over here."

"So what's this about?" she asked, trying frantically to form a plan. She pulled a tissue from her pocket and tossed it down.

"I'm surprised you haven't figured it out. You were always supposed to be smart."

"Wild, you mean." She threw down a couple of coins. Beside her, Dante set down his cell phone, lock picks and wallet, then shoved them across the floor.

Tristan shrugged. "Those stories were easy to spread. The tabloids were always digging for dirt."

He'd made her reputation worse? She shook her head, amazed she could feel any disappointment after everything else he'd done. She hadn't known this man at all. "So explain it to me, Tristan. What's with the disease?"

"Revenge." His gaze locked on Dante's. "Something you know all about, don't you, Fantasma?"

So he'd discovered Dante's identity? She snuck Dante a glance, wondering how he'd take that news. A flush darkened his face. The sinews stood out on his neck. His entire body bristled with barely-restrained fury, and she sensed he was at his limit, close to losing control.

Afraid Tristan would goad him into attacking, she spoke up. "What does that have to do with the counterfeit drugs?"

The prince wiped his forehead on the sleeve of his dinner jacket. And for the first time, she noticed the sweat beading his face, the tremors racking his hands. So he wasn't as calm as he seemed.

"I had a good business going," he said. "The separatists smuggled in the fakes. Gomez laundered the profits for me. I had to give them a cut, but I still made money on the deal. Lots of it."

"Cheating sick people out of the drugs they needed to get well." She couldn't keep the outrage from her voice.

Tristan shrugged.

Repulsed by his callous behavior, she drew back. "So what changed?"

"That bomb blast last month. Those damned separatists tried to assassinate us. I had to punish them for that."

Paloma tilted her head, caught by something in Tristan's voice, something beyond his excitement and nerves. Unable to pinpoint the cause, she shook her head. "You could have given them the independence they wanted. Then they'd leave us alone."

"With the shale oil that region has? Once that comes into full production, I'll be richer than any sheik." Tristan mopped his face again with his sleeve. Then he wobbled for a minute, looking confused, and she realized he was sick. Very sick.

With the virus?

Her pulse accelerating, she looked closer at his face and eyes, searching for the signs. "So where does the disease come in?" she asked, trying to keep his attention on her.

"I couldn't retaliate outright, so Gomez put me in touch with a man he knew."

Beside her Dante shifted his weight. "The Third Crescent terrorist."

"Right." Tristan looked surprised and a little dazed, as if he'd forgotten that Dante was there. "He knew an old Soviet scientist who'd worked in their biological weapons program, Biopreparat. They were brilliant. They engineered the ideal weapon—deadly, contagious, incurable. The perfect killing machine."

"And then?" she asked.

Tristan was trembling harder, the weapon quivering wildly in his hands. Did he have a fever—or was it nerves?

"Gomez arranged the meeting. The terrorist brought a sample."

So that was what they'd seen the terrorist hand him in the hall.

"And my sister?" Dante asked, his voice dangerously flat.

"I needed proof that the sample worked. So I gave her a massive dose. That sped the process up." He looked at Dante again. "I didn't realize she had her cell phone with her. A minor slipup there."

His cold-blooded rendering of the murder shocked her. And in that moment she knew without a doubt he'd intentionally killed their brother Felipe and let her take the blame.

And the irony of it all struck her hard. By dedicating her life to helping Tristan, she'd done more than play the fool and waste herself on an unworthy cause. She'd harmed her country, enabling a madman to become the future ruler and hurt the very people she was trying to protect.

And she realized something else. Tristan's evil nature was not her fault. Despite his clean-cut looks and refined upbringing, he had been born a monster, a freak, some sort of genetic aberration. Nothing she could have done would have changed that fact.

Tristan wiped his nose on his sleeve, leaving a bloody streak across his cheek, and her heart kicked up a beat. He *had* to have the virus. He had the signs. But did he know it? Could she use it to their advantage somehow?

"And the casino owner?" she asked, still stalling for time. "What happened to him?"

"That idiot." Tristan's lip curled. "He panicked. When El Fantasma here started nosing around and asking questions, he was afraid his role in the girl's death would come out. He wanted me to stop the shipment of the virus. He tried to blackmail me." His voice ran with outrage.

"So you killed him."

"No. I was going to after you confiscated the evidence, but he died on his own. One of life's ironies, I suppose."

"He caught the disease."

Tristan shrugged, the man's death apparently no more important to him than a pesky fly's.

"And how about you?" she said carefully. "Aren't you afraid you'll catch it, too?"

"I took the antidote."

She caught Dante's eye and realized he'd recognized the symptoms, too. "Where did you get that?" she asked Tristan.

"The same guy who gave me the sample."

Then the terrorist had double-crossed him. The irony made her want to laugh. But Tristan didn't know he had the disease. And all of a sudden, she knew what she had to do.

But before she could even inhale, Tristan lunged forward and whipped her around. Wedging his arm against her windpipe, he held her fast to his chest, his gun barrel pressed to her head.

"Into the closet," he told Dante. "Right now. Or I'll kill her."

Dante didn't move. His black eyes burned into Tristan's, his rage sparking the air. Paloma didn't breathe, terrified that he wouldn't listen, that he would try to do something heroic and cause Tristan to shoot. But after several tense seconds, Dante walked to the closet and opened the door.

"Get in," Tristan ordered.

His jaw clenched, his eyes deadly, Dante stepped inside.

Then Tristan shoved her toward him. She stumbled, staggered upright and spun around.

And suddenly she'd had enough. Maybe he was going to shoot her. Or maybe she would die of the disease. But she intended to make him suffer before she did. "You do know the symptoms of the disease, don't you, Tristan? Headache, fever, chills. Sound familiar?"

His eyes narrowed, but she forged on. "The flushed skin. The bloodshot eyes. That bloody nose. I'll bet your lower back aches, too."

He bobbled the gun, his eyes flashing with fury and fear. "I don't have it. I took the antidote."

"Your friend gave you a fake." She laughed. "He screwed you, Tristan. You're going to die like Dante's sister. Did you see how she looked when you killed her, the way her skin puffed up? The way she bled? How does it feel to know you're going to die like that? How much do you think it'll hurt?"

Tristan's face turned a mottled red. The veins bulged in his neck. His eyes blazing with murderous intent, he strode toward her and cocked the gun. But Dante reached out, jerked her into the closet behind him and slammed the door. Then he shoved her down to the floor.

Shots broke out. Tristan fired again and again at the door, the deafening sound thundering through her skull. She covered her ears, terrified that the bullets would hit them, unable to breathe with Dante's heavy body smashing her into the floor.

Then, mercifully, the shooting stopped. Silence rang in her ears. Tristan locked the closet door with an ominous click.

And then his footsteps faded away.

"What the hell were you trying to do?" Dante demanded, still lying atop her. "Do you have a death wish? Why did you bait him like that?"

"I thought… I was hoping I could distract him so we could disarm him."

"Distract him?" He shuddered, unable to get the image of Tristan pointing the gun at her out of his head. "He nearly killed you!"

"I know."

The quivering in her voice penetrated his anger, and he struggled to get himself back under control. But the sight of Tristan bearing down on her, that insane rage in his eyes, had taken years off his life. "We were lucky his aim was off," he said, shifting off her. "If he'd shot a few inches lower, we'd both be dead."

He rose to his knees, then helped her to her feet, shoving aside the clothes crowding the space. Bullet holes peppered the door, bringing pinpricks of light into the closet, illustrating just how close to death they'd come.

Inhaling to calm his chaotic pulse, he met her eyes. "Are you all right?"

"Define *all right*."

"Yeah."

It had been one hell of a night so far. And it wasn't over yet.

"Let's get out of here." He twisted the doorknob and pushed. Locked.

"Stand back," he said, then kicked it several times, but the thick door wouldn't budge. He dropped to one knee and examined the lock—a typical pin tumbler, easy enough to pick with the right tools.

Wishing he still had his lock picks, he glanced around. The closet was six feet wide and a few feet deep. A rod ran the length of it, crowded with hangers bearing clothes. He grabbed a couple of wire hangers and removed the shirts, then started straightening the ends.

"What are you going to do?" Paloma asked.

"Pick the lock."

"Can I help?"

"Yeah. Get that pole down."

While he continued straightening the hangers, Paloma lifted the rod from out of its brackets and turned to him. "What now?"

"Here, hold this." He handed her one of the straightened hangers. Then he took the rod, stood it on its end and wrapped the other hanger he'd straightened around it to form a loop. He curved the ends of the wire into a triangle, putting some tension into it to create a spring. Slipping it off the pole, he worked in a few more bends.

Satisfied, he took the other hanger and created a rudimentary tension wrench. "Give me a little space," he said, and she backed up again.

Kneeling, he inserted both tools into the lock and began manipulating the pins. The tumblers broke in quick succession. That done, he rotated the cylinder and opened the door.

"Impressive," Paloma said as they stumbled out. "If we survive this, I'm going to insist my father make you a knight for that."

"We're going to survive, all right." There wasn't a chance in hell he'd let Tristan win—or Paloma die. "You'd better take the lead," he added. "Since you know the way."

"Right." Her eyes somber, she hurried across the chamber to the door. Then they slipped into the hallway, running as fast as they could on the polished stone floor. At the end of the hallway, they reached a wide stone staircase and raced down several flights. "This way," she said, sounding breathless.

Keeping one eye out for trouble, he followed her down another hall. How she could run in her condition, he didn't know. She was injured, exhausted, infected with a deadly virus that had to make her feel like hell. But through sheer determination she sprinted along.

His admiration for her rising, he rushed with her past several bedrooms, then passed through a cavernous room decorated with medieval pendants and swords. After running down another hallway, they stopped at an arched wooden door. Dante swept a nervous gaze behind him, hoping they hadn't triggered any alarms.

"We need to go across the wall walk," Paloma told him, breathing hard. "It's a shortcut to the tower. That will lead us right down to the dining room where the dinner is."

She opened the door and slipped out. His tension building, he followed her into the crisp night air. Then they sprinted across the battlement, their feet thudding on the stones.

The crenellated wall blurred past. The tower loomed ahead. The silver glow from the ground-level spotlights illuminated the stones.

Suddenly a shout broke out from behind. "You! Stop!"

His pulse accelerating, Dante ducked his head and sped up. Praying the guards wouldn't shoot and injure Paloma, he pounded behind her toward the tower door.

Paloma flung open the door and dove inside. Dante followed on her heels just as shots rang out.

Perfect. Now they'd have the entire royal guard in pursuit.

Paloma flew down another hallway, this one lined with portraits in gilded frames. They made it to another wide staircase, and the dull roar of voices arose from the banquet room below. He trailed her down the stairs to the dining room door and stopped.

His breath rasping, Dante peered over her head into an enormous room, where hundreds of people sat at the longest tables he'd ever seen. Huge chandeliers hung from the frescoed ceilings. Murals covered the walls. His gaze went to the raised dais just to the right of the door. The king sat in the center, Tristan on his right. Other dignitaries he didn't recognize sat on either side. Armed guards stood at intervals along the wall.

"What's your plan?" he whispered.

Her worried eyes met his. "I need to reach my father. But Tristan's sitting next to him, and we know that he's got a gun."

"Would he try to shoot you, with all these people around?"

"I don't know. He's desperate, and he'll try to stop me somehow. Unless I can get to the microphone... Then everyone can hear me speak."

Dante shifted his gaze to the podium at the front of the room, and his blood ran cold. "Forget it. You'll be too exposed. He'll have a clear shot from there."

"I don't have a choice. It's the only way to get my father's attention."

"No, it's not. I'll create distraction while you get to the king."

Sudden fear filed her eyes. "No. They'll shoot you if you try."

"I don't care."

"Well, I do! Listen, Dante. You need to find a reporter and give him that disk." She coughed again, a raw, wrenching cough that scared him more than those gunshots had. The virus was progressing.

She was almost out of time.

"Paloma..." His voice broke.

Her bloodshot eyes turned fierce. "Listen to me, Dante. People have to see the truth. Promise me you'll do it if anything happens to me."

His heart raced. A week ago he wouldn't have hesitated. This was everything he'd wanted. He could finally destroy the royal family and achieve his goal, getting justice for his sister's death.

But he didn't care about that now. Desperation surged

inside him, the overpowering need to make sure this woman survived.

Footsteps pounded behind them, and his sense of urgency rose. The guards were nearly here.

Without warning, Paloma bolted into the room, heading toward the podium, and his heart careened to a halt. A loud murmur broke out as people began to notice her rushing down the aisle.

"Arrest the prince!" she shouted suddenly. "He's unleashed a deadly virus. He's trying to kill us all!"

Tristan rose from his seat and whipped out his gun.

A woman screamed. Pandemonium erupted as shocked people lunged beneath their tables and fled toward doors. Dante battled his way into the room, shoving through the frenzied people toward the dais, where the guards had surrounded the king.

Shots barked out. More people shouted and screamed. Praying Paloma hadn't been hit, Dante leaped over a table and charged through the panicked crowd, trying to get at the prince.

Suddenly Tristan came into view. Dante didn't hesitate. He sprinted straight toward him. His eyes wild, Tristan raised his gun and fired. But he was out of ammunition.

Confusion entered his eyes, then fear. He tossed aside the gun but whipped out an aerosol can. "Stop right there!" he shouted. "This contains the virus."

Years of pent-up fury inside him, Dante didn't break his stride. He slammed his fist under the prince's jaw, an undercut that took him off his feet. Tristan hit the wall, then collapsed.

Guards instantly surrounded Dante and grabbed his arms, roughing him up as they handcuffed him. But

Paloma had reached the podium, and her voice rose above the din.

"Stop, everyone! Guards, secure the room. We have a national emergency on our hands. We've uncovered a terrorist plot led by the prince. You need to restrain him right now. But don't get too close. He has Ebola, a deadly, contagious virus that he has unleashed in País Vell."

Shock rippled through the room. More murmurs and cries broke out.

"We need to put an immediate quarantine in place," she continued. "The lives of thousands, even millions of people could be at stake."

The king stood. He wavered on his feet, looking shocked. His gaze went from Tristan, who was lying on the floor, to the gun he'd tossed aside. Then he raised his eyes to Paloma on the podium.

Her face was flushed; her long hair in wild disarray. And then she hiccupped.

And in that moment Dante knew it was too late. She'd missed the opportunity to take the antidote. She'd chosen to sacrifice herself to save her people.

If he had any lingering doubts about her altruism, they'd disappeared. She believed in honor and justice, the qualities her brother had mocked her for. She epitomized everything a leader should be.

And he realized something else. He loved her. Desperately. Frantically. Permanently.

And now she was going to die.

Chapter 14

Desperate for news about Paloma, Dante walked through the gates of the royal hospital a week later and worked his way through the crowds of reporters swarming the grounds. They'd set up their command posts outside the hospital, camping in trailers and tents as they waited for updates about the disease. As the biggest news event in decades, the Ebola-chimera virus had attracted worldwide attention, and journalists had streamed into País Vell from across the globe.

But with the country now in lockdown, they were stuck. All roads in and out of País Vell were closed. No planes were allowed to take off or land. The only aircraft allowed in the restricted airspace were the helicopters bringing in supplies—and even those couldn't touch down.

Dante stepped around a newscaster lugging a video-camera just as a chopper came into view, its rotor blades drumming the air. It hovered over the quarantine area—the building directly behind the main hospital—then started lowering supplies via a longline to the workers waiting below.

He paused, his gaze stalling on the building where the most severe cases, including Paloma, were housed. Three layers of barbed wire walled it off. Armed soldiers patrolled the perimeter, keeping unauthorized personnel away. They'd even installed guard towers at regular intervals, making the compound look more like a maximum security prison than a hospital ward.

Dante sucked in a breath, the thought of Paloma wasting away in that hellish compound driving him wild. He wanted to storm the doors, blast past any barriers and do something, anything, to keep her safe.

The cameraman jostled his shoulder. Dante shook himself out of his daze, then continued walking to the hospital's main entrance and climbed the steps. Paloma had been quarantined since the night of the state dinner. When she'd leave—or whether she'd be alive when she did—no one knew.

Two soldiers wearing protective face masks and brandishing semiautomatic rifles guarded the hospital doors. "We need to see your clearance card," one demanded.

Dante pulled out the card that proved he'd received the antidote and that he was authorized to leave his house. Military vehicles patrolled the country's deserted streets, enforcing the lockdown in effect until the virus's three-week incubation period had passed.

"This way, please." The guard led him inside the building, to the receptionist's desk, and handed her the card.

"I have an appointment with Dr. Sanz," Dante told her. She nodded, only her tired eyes visible behind her mask. She checked her computer, then slid him back his card. "You're clear. Room 105, down the hall to the left."

The guard returned to his post outside. Dante headed down the hall into a scene straight out of a war zone. Doctors shouting orders dashed past. People huddled in the corridors, crying and looking distressed. He glanced into rooms overcrowded with cots. The harsh odor of disinfectant permeated the air.

And if this was bad, he could only imagine the hell in the quarantine ward.

He reached Dr. Sanz's office and knocked. No one answered, but a nurse scurried by.

"I saw him heading this way," she told him, her voice muffled in her mask. "He'll be right here. You can wait inside."

"Thanks." Dante opened the door and went in. He strode to the window facing the back of the hospital, then stared out at the barbed-wire fence, the injustice of it all hitting him hard. Why Paloma had caught the disease and he hadn't, no one could say. It appeared to be a random quirk of fate.

Just as her survival would be. The odds were definitely against it. Last he'd heard, a hundred people had already died.

Including the prince.

Dante hissed, glad there'd been some glimmer of justice in this affair. But as for Paloma... He turned and scanned the room—the doctor's framed diplomas hanging on the walls, the medical textbooks crammed on the shelves. All the education and money in the world couldn't defeat a deadly virus and save the woman he loved.

Dr. Sanz entered his office just then. Dark circles underscored his eyes. His face looked sallow, and his lab coat rumpled, making Dante doubt he'd slept in days. "Dante, it's good to see you."

"Dr. Sanz." He reached out and shook his hand.

"Have a seat." The doctor circled his desk and slumped into his chair. Then he tossed his glasses onto the desk and rubbed his eyes.

"How is she?" Dante asked, sitting down, his eyes glued on the doctor's face.

Dr. Sanz let out a heavy sigh. "Not well. I wish I had better news, but I don't."

Dante's hopes tanked.

The doctor scrubbed his face with his hands, then exhaled. "Coffee? Water?"

"No, thanks."

Dr. Sanz rose, grabbed a plastic bottle of water from a small refrigerator in the corner and unscrewed the cap. After guzzling half the contents, he sat back down. "Unfortunately, she didn't get the antidote in time to stop the disease."

"I know." Thanks to her stubborn insistence on saving her countrymen first.

"We've tried all the experimental drugs, but they haven't worked," the doctor continued. "We're doing everything else we can—keeping her hydrated, maintaining her oxygen and blood levels, replacing the electrolytes and coagulation factors she's lost. We've stitched her arm and treated the secondary infection from the gunshot wound. But frankly, there's nothing else we can do except let the disease run its course."

Dante clenched his jaw, outrage building inside him. "You're saying we just sit here and wait?"

The doctor exhaled again. "We're trying to save her, believe me. But we've lost a hundred and three people so far. We've got close to another hundred actively infected in the quarantine ward. I'm sure there'll be more cases that haven't manifested yet. And the fact is, she's hung on longer than most."

His jaw rigid, Dante rose and paced to the door. He wanted to slam his fist into the wall. Charge into the quarantine area and do something to make her well. The idea of sitting around twiddling his thumbs while Paloma battled for her life went against everything he'd stood for his entire life.

"We need to fight this," he argued. "We can't just do nothing and let it win."

Dr. Sanz sighed. "I know how you feel. Losing any patient is hard, but the princess…" He shook his head. "But there's only so much we can do. We need a miracle now."

A miracle? Dante scoffed, knowing the likelihood of that. A miracle hadn't saved his mother. A miracle hadn't saved his sister. And he'd be damned if he'd rely on divine intervention to save Paloma, too.

"Look," the doctor said, steepling his hands. "This might sound far-fetched, but there's a lot about medicine we don't know. And sometimes, for whatever reason, attitude helps."

Dante stopped and scowled. "What are you saying? That she's given up?"

"This disease has taken its toll on her. She's lost her spirit. She needs hope, something to live for, something that will make her want to fight. If you could give her that…"

"How? Are you going to let me in to see her?"

"I can't. I'm sorry. We can't make any exceptions. The risks are just too high."

"Then how the hell—"

"I don't know." The doctor let out a heavy sigh. "I was

just thinking out loud, I guess." He capped his bottle of water and rose, looking even more weary now. "I'll keep you posted on any news."

Dante's stomach plunged, the resignation in the doctor's voice chilling him even more. "When will we know if she's going to make it?"

"In the next few days. We're in the second week now, when she'll either defervesce, meaning her fever will lessen…"

"Or?"

"Or she'll undergo multi-organ failure and die."

Dante shoved open the hospital door a few minutes later and strode outside, Dr. Sanz's words echoing in his mind. Hope. Paloma needed hope. But how was he supposed to rally her spirits when a hundred people had already died? When he couldn't talk to her, couldn't see her? When he couldn't tell her how much he loved her? When he couldn't explain that even if he couldn't have her, even if they went their separate ways and never saw each other again, he needed to know that she was alive and well in the world?

And that without her, he'd be devastated. Empty. Lost.

Dodging the clusters of reporters, he crossed the lawn, his fury over life's injustices growing with every stride. Unlike her despicable brother, Paloma deserved to survive. She was the most selfless, most courageous person he knew. She'd sacrificed everything for her country, expecting nothing in return. *It wasn't fair.*

"Mr. Quevedo!" A reporter ran up to him and shoved a microphone in his face. A man lugging a huge video camera jogged at her side.

Damn. They'd recognized him.

Trying to ignore them, he sped up. Talking to the media was the last thing he wanted to do right now. They'd hounded him since that night at the castle. They'd camped outside his stonemasonry business, trying every trick they knew to find out where he'd gone. Thankfully, he'd bought the Palacio de los Arcos under a sham corporation's name, so no one could connect it to him, guaranteeing him some peace.

He snorted at that. *Peace. Right.* As if he'd been able to rest while Paloma lay in the hospital, battling for her life.

Several more reporters rushed up. A crowd started to gather, impeding his progress and hurling questions his way.

"Could you tell us about the reception?"

"What's your relationship to the princess?"

"Are you really El Fantasma?"

"Did the princess contribute to her brother's death?"

That did it. Furious, he whipped around. Then he planted his hands on his hips and glared at the burgeoning crowd. They were a damned bunch of vultures, every last one of them—not just these reporters, but the entire population of País Vell—criticizing the most noble person he knew while she lay there dying, all because she'd wanted to save *them*.

And suddenly, he knew what he had to do.

More reporters swarmed around him. Word had spread faster than that virus, bringing throngs of journalists racing his way.

"Mr. Quevedo," someone shouted. "Could I talk to you? We'd like to hear your version of events."

He'd talk, all right. It was time he set the record straight.

The crowd swelled even more. Cameras clicked

and flashed. People held up their cell phones, probably streaming his image live on to the internet. Dante waited until the mob began to hush, wanting maximum exposure for this.

"All right. I'll tell you what happened," he said.

And he did. He told them of Paloma's plan to protect her brother, her loyalty to her family, how she blamed herself for Felipe's death. How she sprang him out of prison, where Tristan had locked him up to hide Lucía's death. He spoke of the blackmail evidence, the prince's ties to Vell Pharmaceuticals, and his counterfeit medicine plot. How he was using the separatists, laundering money in the casino and killing innocent civilians with his fake drugs.

Dante talked about Paloma—about her dedication, her courage. How she'd gone after the truth, even knowing it might harm the monarchy. How she had caught the disease but had knowingly soldiered on, wounded, dying, chased by her brother's guards, relentlessly determined to expose her brother's crimes.

How she'd risked everything, nearly falling in the garderobe chute, only to be held hostage by the murderous prince. About her loyalty and love for the country. How she'd forgone the opportunity to get the antidote that would have saved her so she could prevent innocent people from suffering her fate.

He talked about the exaggerated reports. The way the prince had fed stories to the tabloids, causing the people to despise the one person in the royal family who deserved to lead. And that despite it all, she'd still tried to protect them, even knowing their unfair opinion of her.

Then he admitted that he was El Fantasma. That he'd dedicated his life to destroying the monarchy, and that like everyone else, he'd despised her at first. That he'd believed the frivolous image the tabloids portrayed.

But that she was nothing like he'd first believed. She was courageous. Caring. The best their country had to offer.

And she was the woman he loved.

He stopped. Absolute silence fell over the crowd. The wind whispered in the nearby pines.

He loved her. He'd just shouted it to the universe. But the woman who needed to hear it the most, the one he'd give his life to save, would never know.

His heart shattered, he turned and walked away.

Paloma squinted at the people encircling her bed. At least she assumed they were people and not extraterrestrial beings, although the way she kept fading in and out of consciousness, she wasn't sure. They wore puffy plastic suits, rubber gloves and boots and strange giant head coverings that looked like mutant jungle gear. Inside their helmets they wore goggles and gas masks. Hoses ran from their suits, connecting them to oxygen tanks.

She blinked to clear her vision, then decided she wasn't hallucinating when they didn't disappear. But it was hard to stay focused with the excruciating headache torturing her skull. She'd lost all sense of the day or time.

Hoping desperately to see Dante, she struggled to make out the faces behind the protective helmets. Pairs of worried eyes stared back, the only sound the weird rushing noise as they breathed into their masks.

"I'm not going to make it, am I?" she cracked out.

"Of course you are," a man said, his voice hollow. Still tethered to the oxygen tank, he stepped forward, and she thought she recognized Dr. Sanz. She tried to smile at the stock answer, but it took too much effort to keep her lips curved up. She wondered if she was losing control of her facial muscles in the final stages of the disease.

"We brought you something."

Paloma rolled her eyes toward the new voice. A smaller person stepped forward, a woman carrying a stack of newspapers in her gloved hands. She set them on the tray beside Paloma's bed. Paloma glanced at the top paper, which had a photo of the front of the hospital. Flowers covered the grounds, acres of them, as if someone had created a memorial.

Her heart sank even more. "Did my father die?"

"No, no. He's fine."

"They're for Tristan, then?" She was too exhausted to feel angry at him anymore. She'd gone from rage and resentment to resignation and acceptance. What had happened wasn't her fault. She'd done what she could to help him, but he had an evilness inside him she couldn't prevent. And she wasn't going to waste one more second of her rapidly ebbing life thinking about him.

"No," the nurse said again. "Those flowers are for you. Look at the articles. See?"

Surprised, Paloma turned her attention to the papers again. The nurse picked up the stack, an awkward undertaking with her gloved hands, then flipped through the pile so she could see. Paloma glanced at the headlines, her blurry vision making them hard to read.

"Princess saves her country," the nurse read aloud. "Daring princess risks her life. Truth about the royals revealed."

Paloma blinked. *What on earth?*

"You've become a hero," the nurse said, a smile in her muffled voice. "People are holding candlelight vigils and praying for your recovery. Thousands of people are outside the gates right now. They've even defied the curfew because they want you to know they care."

Thunderstruck, Paloma looked at the doctors ringing the bed. They all nodded. Too overcome to process it all, she raised her hand to her throbbing head.

"We've got something else to show you," Dr. Sanz said. "Something we're sure you'll want to see."

The nurse returned the newspapers to the tray beside the bed. Then she walked over and turned the television on. She popped a DVD into the player, turned up the volume, fumbling a bit with her gloves.

Everyone shifted out of the way, leaving a clear line of vision to the screen. Someone closed the drapes and dimmed the overhead lights. The DVD started up, and suddenly Dante came on the screen. Paloma's heart stumbled to a halt.

He looked thinner, haggard, exhausted. Lines of fatigue creased his face. He hadn't shaven in days, and a dark coat of whiskers covered his iron jaw.

And he was so incredibly handsome, so much like everything she'd ever wanted, that a huge yearning swelled inside her, the desperate need to talk to him, hold him, touch him.

Hot tears sprang to her eyes. Was this the last glimpse she'd have of the man she loved?

She loved Dante. She'd finally come to realize that during her time in the hospital. She loved his courage, his skills, his drive. The protective way he'd tried to shield her from harm. She loved his honor, his integrity. How he'd dedicated his life to helping the downtrodden people, determined to right the wrongs her family had done.

And her one regret was that she hadn't told him. It wouldn't have changed their future. She knew he didn't feel the same about her—and how could he, given her family's past? But she still should have told him the truth.

Reporters pushed and swarmed around him. The camera bobbed and wove, and she rubbed her eyes, hoping the dizziness would pass. Then the picture stabilized, and the camera homed in on his face.

"All right," he announced, and his deep voice rumbled through her heart. "I'll tell you what happened."

The crowd fell still. She stayed riveted to the screen, her emotions a maelstrom inside her, as his dark eyes connected to hers. And then he began to talk. About her. About Tristan. About her family and the blackmail. About the terrible ordeal they'd gone through. And he rallied to her defense.

Her throat turned thick. A huge swell of love cramped her chest. But he still forged on, giving a litany of her good qualities and minimizing his own role in the affair. She blinked back her tears, determined to rectify that if she survived.

But he didn't stop there. He spoke of his upbringing and beliefs, his prejudice against País Vell's nobility. He admitted that he was El Fantasma, that he'd embarked on a crusade to destroy the monarchy—every last one of them, including her.

"But I was wrong," he said, still looking straight into the camera. "And I love her." The words arrowed straight to her heart.

The DVD ended. Her throat was so thick, she could hardly breathe. She looked around and realized everyone had left the room, sensing she needed privacy, no doubt.

Her hands trembling, she picked up the pile of papers, squinting at the photos of the flowers and gifts. She thumbed through the articles—about her, the people, Dante.

And then she caught sight of another newspaper the nurse had tucked under the pile. El Fantasma Loves Princess the headline screamed.

She closed her eyes. An unbearable longing wrenched her heart. Dante loved her. She no longer had any doubts.

He'd given her a gift more precious than anything she believed possible. He'd risked everything—his pride, his freedom, his heart—to tell the truth. And he'd given her back her people's respect.

For the first time she had something worth fighting for. Worth living for. Worth surviving for.

She was going to claim the man she loved.

Chapter 15

"She left the hospital this morning," Miguel said.

Dante grunted in response. Then he flipped over the wooden door he was sanding and centered it on the sawhorses he'd set up in his courtyard to keep the sawdust out of the house.

"I saw it on television," Miguel continued. He leaned back against a pillar and crossed his arms. "You should have seen it. People were throwing flowers and waving flags. The car could hardly get through the crowds."

He'd seen it. He'd been glued to the television like a helpless fool, so crazy in love with her that even a glimpse of the sleek Rolls-Royce Phantom IV, the king's state vehicle, had nearly destroyed his resolve. It had taken every ounce of self-restraint he possessed to keep from barging into the castle and begging her to spend her life with him.

Grabbing hold of his electric sander, he removed

the worn piece of sandpaper from the machine and inserted another. He still couldn't believe she'd recovered. She'd joined the rare 10 percent of cases who'd actually survived Ebola, although the doctors had no idea why. Maybe it was sheer luck. Maybe there'd been enough left of her ravaged immune system to finally fight it off. Or maybe the people had given her hope, rallying her to survive. But a month ago, her fever had finally broken, and she'd started to mend. They'd kept her in the hospital until now to make sure a secondary infection didn't set in, posting daily, sometimes hourly updates on the news.

He'd devoured every one.

He'd been as bad as any addict, clinging to every newscast, reading everything about her he could. He'd hunted for news online, checking articles in every language he understood. And every reminder of her—the photos, the stories, hell, even his own damned house—had been driving him out of his mind.

"There were more crowds waiting at the castle," Miguel said. "You'd have thought it was a coronation. I've never seen anything like it in my life."

Dante set down the sander, then raised his safety goggles with a sigh. "And you're telling me this *why?*"

"So you can go see her."

"See her?" Dante scoffed. "Why would I do that?"

Miguel frowned. "Why wouldn't you?"

"What's the point? She doesn't need me now." She had the king, her adoring subjects. She'd redeemed herself in the eyes of the people and proven her worth. She finally had the royal life she deserved.

"She must want to see you," Miguel argued.

"Well, I sure as hell don't want to see her." It would

only prolong the torture. Better to leave it like this, giving them both a clean break.

"Suit yourself," Miguel finally said, but he didn't look convinced. "But just for the record, I was wrong about her. She has guts. And she's definitely worth fighting for."

"She's the princess. Way out of my league. We worked together to stop that virus, that's all. And now it's done."

Thank God. Before it was over, the virus had claimed over three hundred innocent lives. But there hadn't been any new cases for weeks, so the king had finally lifted the quarantine and allowed travel to resume. Life in the tiny Pyrenees mountain country was returning to normal at last.

He wished he could say the same for his heart.

"I still say you should let her decide that," Miguel said.

Not bothering to answer, Dante snapped his safety goggles back into place.

Miguel straightened and raised his hands. "All right. You win. I'm off to see Rafe. He wants to talk to me about a job. You want to come?"

Dante wasn't fooled. Rafe's fiancée, Gabrielle Ferrer, was Paloma's childhood friend. They'd want to grill him about his feelings for her.

"Too busy." He started up the sander, the loud buzz discouraging further remarks.

Miguel shook his head, mouthed something that looked a lot like *idiota* and strode away.

And for a minute Dante just stood there, the temptation to take Miguel's advice and run to Paloma nearly overpowering his common sense. He trembled with the need to touch her. She'd driven herself so deeply inside him that he longed to plead for her to love him, to let him share her life.

But she had a royal role to play. And he refused to hold her back.

Turning his attention to the door, he put some muscle behind the sander, sending sawdust spraying into the air. *Idiota* or not, his time with Paloma was done.

Now he just had to convince his heart.

Paloma pulled up to Dante's house, parked her borrowed Fiat next to a wrought-iron lamppost and climbed out of the car. It had taken some fancy footwork to escape the paparazzi swarming the castle. She'd worn a wig, snuck out through the workers' entrance and even changed vehicles twice.

Because nothing was going to stop her from seeing the man she loved.

Her nerves thrumming, she hiked up the cobblestone street to Dante's door. The sun had broken through the clouds, enveloping the traumatized country in a soft, healing glow, mimicking their hope that life would march on. She stopped before the wooden door, inhaled to quell the sudden burst of anxiety rising inside her, and lifted her hand to knock.

But the door swung open, and Miguel stepped out. Startled, she took a quick step back. He paused, his own surprise reflected in his gray eyes.

Would he let her in? She knew he didn't care for her. But his mouth curved up, amusement gleaming in his eyes as he held open the door.

"Thank you," she said.

He pushed his glasses higher on the bridge of his nose. "I was glad to hear you recovered."

Taking that as an olive branch that she knew he intended, she smiled. "I appreciate that."

He nodded and started to walk away.

"Miguel?" He turned back. "I'd like to talk to you when you have a chance. About business." She wanted to convince him to use his skills for the crown—and the greater good.

He slashed a smile at her. "We'll see about that."

Yes, they would. She stepped into Dante's courtyard, her own smile fading as she closed the door. This was it. It was time to confront the man she loved—and determine the rest of her life.

She followed the loud buzz of machinery to the center of the courtyard. Her gaze arrowed straight to Dante, and she stopped. He stood beside a long plank balanced on sawhorses, his head bent as he worked. He had his sleeves shoved up. Sawdust floated in the air, speckling his strong arms. Leather work gloves covered his hands.

He bore down on the machine, leaning farther over the plank, concentration etched on his dark face. She took in the wide ledge of his shoulders, the muscles flexing in his back and arms, the tool belt strapped over his faded jeans. And it was all she could do not to leap into his arms and beg him to make wild, passionate love to her right where he stood.

He wore safety goggles over his eyes, ear protectors to block out the noise. His hair was shaggier and longer than the last time she'd seen him, a month ago. She curled her hands, trying to resist the urge to plunge her fingers through that inky hair. Instead, she stood rooted in place, trying to get her emotions for him under control so she didn't blow the only chance she'd have.

All of a sudden he glanced up. He went completely still, the sander still running in his hand, and she couldn't seem to breathe. What was he thinking? Was he happy to see her? Wishing desperately that she could see his eyes behind those goggles, she waited for him to speak.

He turned off the sander and set it down, abrupt silence filling the air. Then he pulled off the goggles and earphones and tossed them onto the door, followed by his leather gloves. His gaze still on her, he crossed his arms, not a hint of his feelings on his face.

Her throat desert dry, she walked toward him across the stones. She stopped as close as she dared beside him, devouring him with her gaze. He'd lost weight. Shadows darkened the skin beneath his eyes. She took in his stubble-covered cheeks, his endearingly crooked nose, and the pressure in her chest increased.

"I figured you wouldn't come to see me," she said.

His eyes flickered. "You figured right."

She wavered, doubts suddenly creeping through her mind. Was that because he didn't want to see her? But no, he loved her. She'd seen the headlines in the paper. She'd heard him confess it to the world.

"So I decided to come here," she continued. "I had things I wanted to say. I...well, first off, I want to thank you. What you did...that speech..." Her mouth wobbled badly, and she cleared her throat. "That's the nicest thing anyone has ever done for me."

"I just told the truth."

"You did more than that. You changed my life."

His eyes softened a fraction. "You did that yourself."

"I don't think so. If it hadn't been for you..." She hugged her arms and sighed. "And just so you know, my father admitted he knew about Tristan's drug smuggling." Which had further disillusioned her about her family. "Or at least he suspected as much. But he didn't want to expose his son, the future king. He thought the monarchy should continue at any cost."

"Typical."

"I know. But after that virus...he's agreed to change

the primogeniture laws. From now on, women can inherit the crown—assuming the people still want a monarchy. It's going up for a referendum next year."

Dante's eyes began to warm. Leaning closer, he reached out and tucked a strand of hair behind her ear, the gentle gesture escalating her pulse. "They'll vote you in. You'll make a great queen."

"Maybe. But even if they do, I won't have as much power. It's time País Vell enters the twenty-first century and makes some reforms. The monarchy will be a lot more symbolic than it is now, assuming it survives."

She had so many reforms she wanted to enact, from bettering their educational system to granting autonomy to Reino Antiguo. But those changes would take time.

And they depended on the peoples' will.

"Listen, Dante." Her voice shook, and she cleared her throat. "I didn't come here only to talk about País Vell."

His eyes suddenly wary, he rocked back on his heels.

"I had a lot of time to think when I was in that hospital. I've wasted so much time—protecting my brother, rebelling against my father's expectations, trying to conform to something I'm not. And I decided that if I survived, I was going to go after what I want." She swallowed, her pulse embarking on a breakneck race. "And what I want is you."

He didn't speak. A completely blank expression fell over his face. And something inside her died.

"I won't blame you if you say no. What my family did to yours...I know you won't ever forget. But I love you, Dante. I know we haven't known each other long, but I do. And when I was lying in that hospital, the only thing I regretted in this whole sordid affair was not telling you that. I vowed I was going to survive so I could let you know."

"Paloma…" Regrets pulled at his voice.

Feeling frantic, she rushed on. "You saved me, Dante. You gave me a reason to survive that awful disease. You said you loved me. Maybe that's changed, but—"

"It hasn't changed." He strode forward and cradled her jaw with his hands, and her heart quivered hard in her chest. "For God's sake, Paloma, how could it? You're everything to me. But I'm a thief. I'm not an aristocrat. I'm exactly the wrong man for you."

"You're the *perfect* man for me. The people respect you. They trust you. They need you. You've been their hero for years. You could help smooth the transition so violence doesn't break out."

She wrapped her arms around his neck and pulled him close. "And more importantly, *I* need you. I mean it, Dante. If the only thing holding you back is my status as a noble, then I'll abdicate the throne. I don't have to be a royal." Her voice turned fierce. "But I *do* need you. And I'm not letting anything stand in our way."

He went stone still. For an eternity he didn't speak. His amazing black eyes held her riveted, the love she felt for him bursting inside.

And then he pulled her tighter against him, exactly where she longed to be. "You're sure?" he asked, his voice suddenly gruff, his eyes searching hers. "Because once you say yes, I'm not going to let you go. I want marriage, kids, all of it. Forever."

"Forever," she breathed. "There's nothing I want more."

His mouth claimed hers, and for the first time in her life a feeling of absolute rightness settled over her world. A happiness she knew would last.

* * * * *

SUSPENSE

COMING NEXT MONTH
AVAILABLE MARCH 27, 2012

#1699 CAVANAUGH'S BODYGUARD
Cavanaugh Justice
Marie Ferrarella

#1700 LAWMAN'S PERFECT SURRENDER
Perfect, Wyoming
Jennifer Morey

#1701 GUARDIAN IN DISGUISE
Conard County: The Next Generation
Rachel Lee

#1702 TEXAS BABY SANCTUARY
Chance, Texas
Linda Conrad

REQUEST YOUR FREE BOOKS!
2 FREE NOVELS PLUS 2 FREE GIFTS!

ROMANTIC
SUSPENSE

Sparked by Danger, Fueled by Passion.

YES! Please send me 2 FREE Harlequin® Romantic Suspense novels and my 2 FREE gifts (gifts are worth about $10). After receiving them, if I don't wish to receive any more books, I can return the shipping statement marked "cancel." If I don't cancel, I will receive 4 brand-new novels every month and be billed just $4.49 per book in the U.S. or $5.24 per book in Canada. That's a saving of at least 14% off the cover price! It's quite a bargain! Shipping and handling is just 50¢ per book in the U.S. and 75¢ per book in Canada.* I understand that accepting the 2 free books and gifts places me under no obligation to buy anything. I can always return a shipment and cancel at any time. Even if I never buy another book, the two free books and gifts are mine to keep forever.

240/340 HDN FEFR

Name _____ (PLEASE PRINT) _____

Address _____ Apt. # _____

City _____ State/Prov. _____ Zip/Postal Code _____

Signature (if under 18, a parent or guardian must sign) _____

Mail to the **Reader Service:**
IN U.S.A.: P.O. Box 1867, Buffalo, NY 14240-1867
IN CANADA: P.O. Box 609, Fort Erie, Ontario L2A 5X3

Not valid for current subscribers to Harlequin Romantic Suspense books.

Want to try two free books from another line?
Call 1-800-873-8635 or visit www.ReaderService.com.

* Terms and prices subject to change without notice. Prices do not include applicable taxes. Sales tax applicable in N.Y. Canadian residents will be charged applicable taxes. Offer not valid in Quebec. This offer is limited to one order per household. All orders subject to credit approval. Credit or debit balances in a customer's account(s) may be offset by any other outstanding balance owed by or to the customer. Please allow 4 to 6 weeks for delivery. Offer available while quantities last.

Your Privacy—The Reader Service is committed to protecting your privacy. Our Privacy Policy is available online at www.ReaderService.com or upon request from the Reader Service.

We make a portion of our mailing list available to reputable third parties that offer products we believe may interest you. If you prefer that we not exchange your name with third parties, or if you wish to clarify or modify your communication preferences, please visit us at www.ReaderService.com/consumerschoice or write to us at Reader Service Preference Service, P.O. Box 9062, Buffalo, NY 14269. Include your complete name and address.

HRS11B

Taft Bowman knew he'd ruined any chance he'd had for happiness with Laura Pendleton when he drove her away years ago...and into the arms of another man, thousands of miles away. Now she was back, a widow with two small children...and despite himself, he was starting to believe in second chances.

Harlequin Special® Edition® presents a new installment in USA TODAY *bestselling author RaeAnne Thayne's miniseries,* THE COWBOYS OF COLD CREEK.

Enjoy a sneak peek of
A COLD CREEK REUNION

Available April 2012 from Harlequin® Special Edition®

A younger woman stood there, and from this distance he had only a strange impression, as though she was somehow standing on an island of calm amid the chaos of the scene, the flashing lights of the emergency vehicles, shouts between his crew members, the excited buzz of the crowd.

And then the woman turned and he just about tripped over a snaking fire hose somebody shouldn't have left there.

Laura.

He froze, and for the first time in fifteen years as a firefighter, he forgot about the incident, his mission, just what the hell he was doing here.

Laura.

Ten years. He hadn't seen her in all that time, since the week before their wedding when she had given him back his ring and left town. Not just town. She had left the whole damn country, as if she couldn't run far enough to get away from him.

Some part of him desperately wanted to think he had made some kind of mistake. It couldn't be her. That was just some other slender woman with a long sweep of honey-blond hair and big, blue, unforgettable eyes. But no. It was definitely Laura. Sweet and lovely.

Not his.

He was going to have to go over there and talk to her. He didn't want to. He wanted to stand there and pretend he hadn't seen her. But he was the fire chief. He couldn't hide out just because he had a painful history with the daughter of the property owner.

Sometimes he hated his job.

Will Taft and Laura be able to make the years recede...or is the gulf between them too broad to ever cross?

Find out in
A COLD CREEK REUNION
Available April 2012 from Harlequin® Special Edition®
wherever books are sold.

**Celebrate the 30th anniversary
of Harlequin® Special Edition® with a bonus story
included in each Special Edition® book in April!**

us bear. He has taken away our fears and worries, and has given us everything we need. These blessings from God should make us strong to bear the trials during the rest of our life journey.

We cannot help thinking about the trials and tests we will face before the end of the world. But we can look back as well as forward and say, "The Lord has helped us all the way." "As your days, so shall your strength be" (Deuteronomy 33:25, RSV). The trials will not be greater than the strength God will give us. So let us take up our work where we find it, believing we will be strong enough to meet whatever comes.

Someday the gates of heaven will be thrown open to welcome God's children. From the lips of the King of glory will fall a blessing like rich music: "Come, you that are blessed by my Father! Come and possess the kingdom which has been prepared for you ever since the creation of the world" (Matthew 25:34).

The redeemed will be welcomed to the home that Jesus is preparing for them. In heaven there will be no wicked people. The friends of the redeemed will be people who have overcome Satan through divine grace and have formed perfect characters. Every desire to sin will have been taken away by the blood of Christ. The redeemed will shine with Christ's glory, which is much brighter than the sun. And what is more, the beauty of His character will also shine out through them. They will stand without fault before God and will have the same blessings as the angels.

A beautiful heavenly home is ready for the redeemed. "Will you gain anything if you win the whole world but lose your life?" (Matthew 16:26). A person may be poor now, but in the gift of eternal life he owns greater wealth than the world can ever give. A person redeemed by Jesus, made clean from all sin, and serving God is of more value than the whole world. There is joy in heaven before God over every person that is redeemed. This joy makes the heavenly angels sing holy songs of victory.